The Cowboy and the Nanny

 Horseshoe Home Ranch

LIZ ISAACSON

ISBN-13: 978-1-63876-241-6

"From the end of the earth will I cry unto thee, when my heart is overwhelmed: lead me to the rock that is higher than I."

— PSALMS 61:2

CHAPTER 1

The barn door banged open as Gil, one of the male counselors, burst through it. "Owen, there's a fight we need your help with." He didn't wait to see if Owen would come. He did. Owen Carr had the most experience with the troubled boys at Silver Creek, having worked with the at-risk boys for the past seven years, since he'd been at the part therapeutic riding center, part rehabilitation center.

He left the saddles where they were on the bench, left the horses in the stall, left everything, and followed Gil at a run. "Is it one of my boys?" he called after the other man.

"Stanley! He has a weapon."

Owen's heart sped at the same time he groaned. He increased his speed, leaving behind the horse barn and stalls, the cabin where he used to live, and the hay barn. He tore around the corner of the building to find a crowd of boys circling two others.

"Move," he called. "Now, boys. Move aside." No one dared disobey Owen when he spoke, whether it was in his normal quiet way or in the intense bark he used now. The boys parted to reveal Stanley holding a homemade knife.

"Stanley," Owen said. "Drop it right now." The stick looked to have a piece of metal from a belt or a saddle strap attached to the end of it. And it glinted sharply in the September sun.

Stanley glanced from the other boy to Owen. "Mister Carr—" He swallowed.

Owen strode forward, his nerves already preparing to be hurt. They fired on all cylinders as he got closer and closer to Stanley. He really didn't have time for this. He'd been fifteen minutes away from finishing his work in the barn and leaving. He had an appointment to keep.

"Give me the knife, Stanley." Owen stopped five feet from the teen, whose dark eyes seemed wild and scared. "This doesn't end well if someone gets hurt. You can come over to the cabin and tell me what happened." Owen met the other boy's eyes, and he didn't look nearly as afraid as Stanley did. Owen settled his weight on his back foot. "What's goin' on?"

"He said he knew my sister," Stanley said, and Owen cringed. Stanley was fiercely protective of his family, and he hasn't yet grasped that it didn't matter what anyone else said about them. "Said she was easy, said all his friends had kissed her."

"So you thought you'd make 'im bleed over somethin' that ain't true?" Owen kept the sigh he wanted to add from escaping. "Give me the knife, Stanley. This boy isn't worth it." He glared at the other boy now, who wore a smirk. He'd gotten exactly what he wanted, and Owen hoped Stanley wouldn't suffer too much because of it.

Stanley inched toward Owen until Owen could wrap his fingers around the boy's wrist. He did, as tight as he dared, and Stanley dropped the knife. Owen stomped on it, kept his grip on his boy, and turned to the crowd. "Go on, now. Get back to your chores." He twisted toward the other boy. "You're comin' with me."

"You're not my counselor."

Owen growled and took two steps toward the boy, who flinched away. Satisfied, Owen pushed his cowboy hat lower over his eyes. "Come on." He spied Dr. Richards hurrying across the lawn, and he held his ground as the crowd dispersed.

"Owen," Dr. Richards panted. "What's happened?"

"Stanley was gettin' teased and he fashioned some weapon." He moved his boot to reveal the makeshift knife. "To teach this other boy a lesson. I'll let you handle him."

Dr. Richards turned his gaze on the other boy and frowned. "Gerard." His eyes blazed with anger. "You have to stop this." He turned and headed back toward his office, the other boy in tow.

"My cabin," Owen said, nudging Stanley in that direction.

"I thought you moved out."

"I did." Owen had lived there so long, he'd always think of it as his. Dr. Richards hadn't given it to anyone else, because Owen still oversaw the horses, still worked with the at-risk boys. His hours were the same, and Dr. Richards simply assigned the at-risk boys to his on-call counselors for after-hours emergencies.

Because Marie had changed everything.

The fight left Owen's body and he gave that sigh he'd held back earlier. "You know, you're makin' me late, Stanley." He redirected him toward the barn. "So you get to do the clean-up chores in the barn."

"I'm sorry, Owen." Stanley sounded remorseful too. He always did, once he actually calmed down enough to think rationally.

"It's Mister Carr. And you need to work on your impulse control," Owen said as he released the boy into the barn. "Oil the saddles and hang them up. All the reins go up there too. And both those horses need to be fed and brushed down."

Owen leaned against the doorframe while Stanley got to work. It would take the boy twice as long as it took Owen, and he'd be even later. But he couldn't abandon Stanley—he wouldn't. Not when he barely had anyone to hang on to.

"What're you gonna be late for, Mister Carr?"

Owen pushed away from the wall and reached for the reins as Stanley finished the last saddle. "Remember how I have my niece living with me now?"

"Marie, sure."

"Well, because I'm here with you guys so much, I need help takin' care of her." Everything in him twisted and wound tight. He'd always loved Marie, the daughter of his

4

only sister. He'd agreed to be her guardian if anything happened to her sister and her husband. He'd just never expected anything to actually happen to them.

Owen's life had changed a lot in the past six months. He'd become a father and an only child because of an ice storm and a horrible, horrible car accident.

He pushed away the memories that threatened to drown him every time he let his mind linger on them too long. "I'm hirin' a nanny to help out." He checked his watch. "And I'm supposed to meet with her in ten minutes."

Because an eight-year-old girl couldn't live fifteen yards from half a dozen troubled boys who had landed at Silver Creek because of their tendencies to mix weapons with drugs, Owen had found a cottage in a nice neighborhood— fifteen minutes from Silver Creek. No matter how he sliced it, he was going to be late.

He'd gotten Marie a simple cell phone the very first day she'd come to live with him. He called her and told her he'd be several minutes late. "Is that okay, Marie? Maybe you can ask the lady a few questions." He smiled despite himself, despite the fact that he had very little in his life to smile about. No matter what, Marie did bring a smile to his face. So blonde her hair was almost white, with deep blue eyes like his sister's. Like his.

"I can do it, Owen."

"I shouldn't be too long." He turned when Stanley walked Ole Red past him. Only one horse remained, and if Owen helped, he could be on the road in under ten minutes. He hung up with Marie and grabbed a curry comb.

"Now, Stanley, you got any other weapons?"

"No, sir."

"I'm gonna have to search your things. You know that, right?"

"Yes, sir." Regret laced his words. "I really am sorry, Owen."

Owen didn't correct him this time. He didn't mind being more casual with his boys. He wanted—needed—them to trust him. They finished in the barn, and Owen searched Stanley's belongings. He filed the incident paperwork, and asked Dr. Richards if he could meet with him in the morning, that he needed to get home to Marie.

Dr. Richard's waved him out of the office, and Owen hurried to his truck. A pang of longing for his old life reared up as he left the parking lot. Before Marie, after a day like today, Owen would retreat to his cabin and make himself a sandwich. Then he'd sit on the front porch with his guitar and sing until all his boys came and sat on the steps with him.

He'd talk to them, and they'd listen, and the bond between them would strengthen until incidents like this didn't happen anymore. He'd lost that when he'd moved out. He didn't need to play on the porch every night—though he usually did. But after days like today, he did—which was why he needed a nanny for Marie.

A black sedan sat in his driveway, so he parked on the street. He hadn't yet gotten out of his truck when Marie squealed. She appeared around the side of the house, a huge smile on her face. Owen's dog followed, his tongue lagging out of his mouth.

Owen smiled at the two of them as Tar Baby overtook Marie and knocked her to the ground. They wrestled amidst Marie's laughter as a tall, slim woman came from the backyard as well.

She moved with the grace of someone who knew exactly where to put their feet. Her long, dark hair was streaked with blonde, and her hazel eyes glinted with happiness as she watched the girl and dog in front of her.

Owen's heart skipped several beats and he seemed frozen to the seat. This woman's beauty exceeded any he'd met before, and she seemed vaguely familiar.

He managed to slide out of the truck and start to cross the lawn. "Hey," he called, his voice finally thawing. It sounded semi-normal too, thank goodness. He hadn't had the best of luck in the dating department, not that he'd tried that hard—especially after his return to Gold Valley several years ago.

He'd ruined everything with his high school girlfriend when he'd left town the day after their graduation, and then he'd had his heart broken by a woman in Nashville. So no, he hadn't tried that hard at all since coming home and starting at Silver Creek.

"C'mon Tar Baby." The black cocker spaniel leapt away from a still-giggling Marie. "Hey, sweetheart." He bent over and picked up the little girl, hugging her tight. His momma had told him to show Marie how much he loved her, that he was glad to have her living with him. He tried to tell her he loved her, and he gave her as much affection as he could muster. "Did you interview the nice lady?" He cut the woman a glance. "Sorry I'm late."

The woman's eyes had flecks of gold in them, and they hooked Owen and held him fast. "Do I know you?"

"Of course you do, Owen." She gave a nervous laugh. "I'm Natalie Lower."

The name reverberated through his head, and old wounds opened, hurt, and bled. He shook his head real slow. "No. No, you said your name was Natalie Ringold."

"Well, it is." She looked like she'd been doused with ice water. "I got married nine years ago."

The internal injuries widened, and the pain knifing through Owen felt as hot as fire. "Married?"

"Lasted less than a year, Owen. Honestly, don't you know any of the town gossip?" She smiled, but it was full of nerves and lasted only a moment.

"Only been back for the last seven years." His voice sounded like he was speaking into a tin can. "And no, I've only actually lived in town for six months." He set Marie on her feet. "Go play with Tar Baby, sweetheart. Go on, Tar Baby." The girl ran off with the dog, leaving Owen to talk with the high school sweetheart he'd left twelve years ago.

All he could do was pray, and he didn't even know for what. Only that he'd definitely need the help of the Lord to make it through the next few minutes.

Natalie stared at Owen, the same Owen Carr she'd fallen in love with all those years ago. So much of him was the same —that fire in those navy eyes. That black cowboy hat. Those wide shoulders, the day-old scruff on his chin, the cowboy boots he had to have specially made because his feet were so large.

The only thing missing was his guitar.

"I kept up with you," she said, her voice on the edge of shaking. "They played your songs all over the country."

His expression stormed and his teeth clenched. "That's over now." He stepped past her toward the front steps.

She scrambled after him, her stomach quaking. "You had a record deal, Owen. You got what you wanted. What you left—" She cut herself off before she could finish the sentence. He heard what she'd say anyway. *You got what you wanted when you left me here to pursue your own dreams.*

He'd promised her he'd come back. Promised he'd come back and take her to Nashville with him. And he might have, but she'd gotten married about the same time his first single hit the country music charts. She'd known while dating Jeremiah that she shouldn't, but she'd accepted his diamond and gone through the whole charade of a wedding anyway.

Why, she wasn't sure. But now, following Owen into his house, she knew why. She'd been so lonely, so empty, without Owen. She'd simply wanted someone, and it didn't seem to matter who.

She was older now. While she still felt lonely most days, and empty even after she ate, she didn't turn to a hand-

9

some face to fill her life. She'd turned to serving the community on the library board, teaching cooking classes through the church's community program, and finishing her dance degree. She taught ballet to little boys and girls, and she loved it. But she needed more. Thus, why she'd applied for this job, though she'd known exactly who Owen Carr was and how he came to need a nanny. She'd been back in Gold Valley for two years, and she knew all the gossip.

"Marie's great," she said once she'd closed the door behind her. "I'd love to help you with her."

He kept his back to her as he moved into the kitchen and opened the fridge. "Want somethin' to drink?" He pulled out two bottles of water.

She nodded and accepted the water. "I can help in the mornings, like you said. I can be here after school. She can come over to the dance studio with me. I teach ballet there, and you can pick her up whenever you're done."

"She doesn't dance."

"Well, maybe she'd like to." Natalie tucked her hair behind her ear, suddenly aware of the weight of his gaze. That hadn't changed either. The way his muscles rippled under his skin certainly had, as well as the way he collected his emotions close and kept his temper in check. "I teach from four to seven on Mondays and Tuesdays. The other afternoons, I can just pick her up from school and bring her home, make dinner." She waved her hand. "Whatever else you need around here."

He didn't seem to need much, but dirty dishes did wait

in the sink, and dust seemed to have taken up permanent residence on the shelves.

He regarded her with those gorgeous eyes. The very same ones that had drank her up when they'd sat next to each other at a swim meet, which she'd attended to watch her brother. He'd come to support one of his friends. Though they'd grown up together in Gold Valley, she'd never *seen* him until that meet. They started spending a lot of time together after that, and by their senior year, she'd fallen in love with him.

He'd always talked about going to Nashville and becoming a country star. His voice was smooth and even and beautiful, and the man could play a guitar like he was born to do exactly that. The fact that he'd achieved his dreams, even if it was only one record, one single that went to the top of the charts, didn't matter. He'd done it.

"Natalie—" he started.

"I need this job, Owen." She wrung her hands until she realized she was doing it. She rubbed her palms along her thighs. "Marie likes me. Ask her."

He blinked at her. Drained his water, never taking his eyes from hers. "Fine. I will." He tossed the empty water bottle in the sink and moved toward the back door, a perfect storm of Owen Carr that made Natalie want to soothe him, the way she often had. Kiss him, the way she often had. Whisper to him that she loved him, the way she often had.

He'd soothed her too. Kissed her. Told her he loved her. But in the end, none of that had been enough. He'd still left.

She followed him as far as the deck on the back of the house, watched while he scrubbed behind his dog's ears and spoke to Marie. The little girl brightened and nodded, and Owen's shoulders fell. A surge of satisfaction moved through Natalie.

She'd wondered how she could reinsert herself into Owen's life. She'd seen him from a distance since she'd come back to Gold Valley. Seen him at church. Heard about his work at Silver Creek. And everyone had rallied around him when his sister died. His parents still lived in town, but Tasha's will had specified Owen as Marie's legal guardian, and he'd done what was necessary.

When she'd seen his ad for a nanny, she'd applied, beyond hopeful. *Please let this be our second chance,* she prayed as he turned back to her. She couldn't read his expression under his cowboy hat from this distance, but as he stalked closer, she saw the indecision, the anger, the pain.

"She likes you," he clipped out as he passed.

"So can I have the job?" She hated seeing his retreating back as he marched into the house and around the corner into the kitchen. She'd seen enough of him walking away from her to last a lifetime.

"I'll let you know," he said. "I have other interviews still to do."

She entered the kitchen to find him peering into the freezer. "I teach cooking classes at the church," she said. "I can make dinner. Give you a sample of what a meal might taste like when you get home from work."

"That's not necessary."

Desperation darted through Natalie. "Owen—"

"I'm real sorry," he blurted. "Okay? I'm sorry I left and never came back."

His apology brought warmth to her soul. "It's over," she said. "The past. Something that happened twelve years ago."

He closed the freezer and looked right at her. He'd always been able to see past what she said to get to the root of how she really felt. "Are you over it?"

"I—"

"Because I'm not." Agony shone in his eyes for one, two, three seconds before he erased it. "But I do want you to know I'm sorry."

She touched his arm, and lightning sparked at the skin-to-skin contact, causing her to jerk back. "I am too, Owen."

"Nothin' for you to be sorry about." He backed into the living room. "I'll let you know about the job."

"When?"

"Soon."

"How many more interviews do you have?"

"Three."

He'd resorted to one-word answers, so she nodded, ducked her head, and slipped out the front door.

CHAPTER 2

*N*atalie exhaled as she pulled into her own driveway, only a five-minute drive from Owen's. Had she known, she would've taken two lefts to drive by his place more often. She dismissed the thought. No, she wouldn't have. She wasn't so hung up on him that she'd stalk him.

In fact, though she needed the job, she wasn't sure she actually wanted it. Sure, she thought Owen was as handsome as ever. He radiated strength and warmth from his very person. And the thought of kissing him again sent excitement through her in the form of tremors. On some level, she still loved him. She wondered if she always would, he being her first love and all.

But she didn't like the trapped feelings she'd felt in every relationship since. She didn't like wondering what mood her boyfriend or husband would be in when she walked through the door. With Jeremiah, he saved his worst self for her, it seemed.

He couldn't treat his co-workers badly, but he could his wife. He took so much time off work, he bounced from job to job. He was a good person, constantly thinking of others and doing little things to make their lives brighter. He wrote kind cards and bought gifts—for everyone except her. She'd felt neglected and overlooked from the very first time they'd gone out.

And she'd never known who or what was waiting behind the closed door of their home on the north end of town. She knew the sick feeling deep in the gut of not wanting to go home. And she'd vowed that she'd never endure that kind of anxiety again.

Natalie liked knowing that behind her closed door sat her cat, Cranberry, her dirty cereal bowl from that morning, and the running shoes she'd worn to the gym that morning lying by the front door.

She got out of the car and stretched her back in the waning autumn light. She had liked Marie, and that was who this job was all about. She climbed the front steps to her house and entered the unlocked door. Sure enough, Cranberry mewed as she wound through Natalie's legs and her eyes fell on the shoes by the door.

She took a deep breath and released it, none of the anxiety she'd experienced previously inside her. After her failed marriage, Natalie had finished her dance degree and taken every culinary course the local vocational school offered. In her two-bedroom house, she was able to do the two things she loved most: dancing and cooking. They both kept the thoughts of failure, the ever-looming loneliness, at bay.

She pulled the flank steak from the fridge and set about sharpening her knife. Twenty minutes later, she had razor-thin slices of beef marinating in soy and ginger and garlic. She set her hands to chopping peppers, onions, and broccoli as her mind whirred through her upcoming pie classes at the church.

She needed to meet with the new activity director and make sure she had the budget to do pecan pie. She missed Megan, the previous director. Natalie had made Megan's wedding cake, and the whole affair was only two weeks old. She and her new husband—a cowhand from Horseshoe Home Ranch—had flown off to a tropical destination, and then they were moving to Utah.

Natalie needed to confirm times for the classes. Her cooking lessons were some of the more popular ones offered at the church, and she often did mid-day classes for the older generations and evening times were reserved for working people.

She set the broccoli to steam and reached for her phone. "Maureen," she said when the activity director for the church answered. "When can I come talk to you about the upcoming cooking classes?"

"What does tomorrow look like for you?"

Tomorrow was wide open for Natalie—a real problem if she wanted to keep eating flank steak and paying her mortgage. She'd been scraping by for years, teaching dance and doing freelance web design. But she hated the online work —didn't quite have the discipline needed to set her own hours and work from home.

With an appointment set for ten a.m., Natalie finished putting together her beef and broccoli dish and sat down at her eat-in kitchen table. She turned on her Internet radio and enjoyed her meal for one. Well, she enjoyed it as much as she could alone. Her traitorous thoughts kept drifting to Owen, and if he'd even fit at the only other chair at the table. She had her doubts.

"Get over him," she muttered to herself as she moved down the hall and changed into a leotard. While lacing her ballet shoes, a memory she'd long abandoned slammed into her head.

Her senior year, she'd danced the part of the Sugar Plum Fairy in her studio's production of The Nutcracker. Owen had come—he always attended her concerts—and brought her a nutcracker and a single red rose.

She crossed the hall to her bedroom, where that nutcracker sat on her dresser. She'd dried the rose, but she wasn't sure where it was now. Jeremiah had asked her about the nutcracker several times, and she'd said it had senti-mental value. She'd passed it several times everyday, and yet she hadn't seized onto the memory of where it had come from.

Now, she ran her fingertips along the base and up the legs. The nutcracker wore a festive green suit coat, and a smile stole across her face. Owen had said, "I would never wear that color, but he looks nice, don't you think?"

She'd taken the gift and embraced the boy she loved.

He's not a boy anymore, she thought as she turned abruptly away from the nutcracker. She went back into her dance studio and moved to the barre. By concentrating on each muscle in her leg, in each slow, precise movement ballet required, she was able to drive Owen from her mind.

At least for an hour.

———

Owen pulled the turkey steaks off the heat and set the pan on the granite cutting board. "Marie," he called. "Time to eat."

The girl came down the hall from her room, a pencil in her hand.

"Got your homework done?" he asked as he got two plates out of the cupboard. "Mashed potatoes tonight." He grinned at her, though he didn't feel an ounce of joy in his body. "Your favorite."

"Did you make gravy?"

He scoffed. "Did I make gravy." He put the pan next to the turkey steaks. "Of course I made gravy." He leaned against the counter, the early hour at which he woke catching up to him. "You know, your mom loved gravy. She used to put it on everything. I even saw her ladle it over spaghetti once."

Marie smiled, and she didn't look like quite as washed out. "I know, Uncle Owen. You told me last time we had turkey steaks."

"Oh. Well." He busied himself getting out silverware and pulling the canned beans from the microwave. "Let's eat, and then I'll look at your homework." He stifled a yawn and served Marie. He'd learned to listen to her talk if she wanted to, but he didn't press her to. He asked her about school, her teacher, the neighbor he'd been using as a nanny since school had started a couple of weeks ago.

She wandered down the hall after dinner, leaving Owen to himself. With shorter days approaching, he felt tired earlier than normal. Or maybe that was just because of the reappearance of Natalie Lower in his life.

He'd always, always regretted cutting her out of his life in the first place. He had few regrets in his life, but that one topped the list. No matter the success he'd enjoyed in Nashville, he shouldn't have left her the way he did. At least he'd been able to apologize, finally.

Her golden eyes played tricks on his heart all night, making him toss and turn until visions of his once-relationship with Nat drove him from bed at five a.m. He arrived at Silver Creek by five-forty-five in time to wake his boys for their six o'clock equine chores. His at-risk boys took exclusive care of the horses, something he'd insisted on from the day he'd started at the center.

He knew the healing power of horses, something he'd experienced on a deeply personal level at a horse ranch in Nashville before he'd returned to Gold Valley. Before waking the boys, he opened the barn and walked down the aisle. His favored horse was Ole Red, and Owen only allowed certain boys to work with her.

A sorrel-colored horse, Ole Red had a black tail and mane that Owen ran his fingers through as the horse nosed his shoulder. "Mornin'," Owen said in the soft voice he reserved just for his animals and his boys. He wasn't soft-spoken, but he didn't need to bluster and yell to get his way. His height had always helped establish his power with the boys, and his no-nonsense attitude achieved the rest.

He thought of the tired eyes of his neighbor when he'd knocked on the door that morning to deposit a sleepy Marie on her couch. It would be so much better to have someone come to his house so Marie could sleep properly until it was time to go to school. He'd had an additional interview the previous evening, but Marie had said, "She smells like that oil you rub into your boots." She'd wrinkled her nose, and Owen had crossed the woman off his list.

He had two more interviews that evening, but he wondered if maybe he should just call Nat and ask her to pick Marie up from school. She'd have dinner ready when he got home....

His mind played tug-of-war with itself as he unlocked and entered the boy's cabin. "Time to get up, boys," he called, clanging the rod through the triangle that served as an alarm clock. Groans and moans met his ears, but his boys got themselves up and in line.

"Trevor and Marcos, you're on feed," Owen said, moving down the line. "Stanley, saddles and tack. Guy and Cory, hay barn. Jesus, the last three stalls on the north end need to be shoveled out and fresh straw put down." He looked down the line, a rush of admiration for these boys pulling through him. "Breakfast at seven, right back here. I don't want to smell horse on you while we're eating."

"No, sir," they chanted.

"Go on then."

His boys set about getting dressed and heading out to their chores. Owen waited until they'd all exited the building, then he joined them in the barn, where Stanley had switched on the radio. Owen made them listen to the morning news and talk radio while they worked, claiming they needed to know a world still existed beyond Silver Creek. A world they were expected to return to, live in, contribute to.

He went around and spoke to each boy, asking them specific questions about their lives, their struggles. They saw a professional psychiatrist, but they bonded with Owen and he often got more out of them than the doctors did.

"Heard from your dad yet?" he asked Trevor when he got to the boy.

"Yeah, he's coming next week. Doctor Richards said we can go to the football game." Trevor flashed him a grin. "Thanks for setting it up, Owen."

Owen clapped Trevor on the shoulder. "You're a great kid, Trevor. Happy to do it."

Owen wished he had someone to tell him he was great when he'd failed. When he'd tried to claw his way back to the surface. He'd achieved great success in Nashville, he knew. For every record made, there were probably fifty artists turned away.

One hit wonder, ran through his head. He'd loved every

song on his first album. He'd written every one right from his heart. Thankfully, one of them other people had connected to. He shouldn't have asked for more. Shouldn't have expected more.

But he had, and those unrealized dreams tainted the success he'd enjoyed down south. That combined with Clarissa's quick exit from his life, and Owen had a hard time remembering anything good associated with his five years in Nashville.

Taking a chance, the way he did with his boys, the way he had when he'd packed a single bag of clothes and all the money he'd saved from mowing lawns in high school and headed a thousand miles across the country, Owen pulled out his phone. Instead of calling, he sent a text to Natalie.

Can you get Marie after school today? Maybe we can do a trial day.

He shoved his phone back in his pocket and checked on Guy and Cory in the hay barn. The boys over there tended to go back to sleep or make a mess of the hay if Owen didn't make it a habit to stick his head in and make sure they were working.

His phone buzzed before he'd taken more than two steps. Natalie had answered already, and Owen was impressed she was up this early. She'd never been a morning person that he remembered.

"She's not the same person you knew at all," he muttered as he read her text.

Sure! She's at Lincoln Elementary, right? That's what she said last night. She's done at 3:15?

23

Right, he typed. *Lincoln Elementary at 3:15. I should be home about 5.* His thumb hovered over the send button before he pressed it. He added, *Thanks, Nat,* and sent that too.

No problem.

Relief washed through him as he sent a message to his neighbor that she didn't need to go down the block to the bus stop to get Marie. He asked her to please tell Marie that Natalie would be picking her up after school, much happier with the day's situation than anything else he'd arranged for the girl.

No one's called me Nat since high school. Natalie's text burned his retinas—another reminder of how much she'd changed.

Sorry. I didn't know.

Just another reminder of what he didn't know about her, and a creeping thought settled in his mind. He wanted to know all about the new Natalie Ringold.

It's fine. She inserted a smiley face and then said, *See you tonight.*

For the first time since Tasha's death, since Marie came to live with him, since Owen had been forced to leave his cabin, he felt a measure of peace slip into his system. He realized he had something worthwhile to look forward to, and he was a bit shocked, scared, spooked that he felt that way because of Natalie.

CHAPTER 3

*O*wen pulled into his driveway just after five o'clock, noting Natalie's black car leaned toward the luxury side of things. He got out of his decade-old truck and gave her a pat on the hood as he headed toward the front door.

"Evenin'," he called as he entered. The house seemed quiet. Too quiet. He paused in shrugging out of his jacket when he smelled the evidence that someone had definitely been here cooking. The air smelled like roasted meat and butter, fresh bread and salt. He took a deep breath, a thread of pleasure passing through him. Dinner he didn't have to make. Pure heaven.

"Stop!" The back door slammed into the wall as Tar Baby skidded through the opening and onto the wood floors.

"No, you devil!" Natalie appeared a moment later, her hair flying wildly around her face. "You can't dig in the mud and then run away! You'll get—" She stopped mid-sentence when she spied Owen leaning against the wall that marked the beginning of the hallway. Tar Baby sat at his feet, dripping mud from his snout.

Owen looked from a semi-muddy woman to an even muddier dog. "Where's Marie?" he asked, fearing the worst. He wanted to reach down and pat the dog hello, but he didn't want mud—and who knew what else—on his already dirty hands.

Natalie glanced over her shoulder. "She's, uh...cleaning up." She wiped her hands together with a look of disgust and then held them out in front of her like they were covered in slime.

"Cleaning what up?" Owen started toward the back door, which still stood open.

Natalie moved to block him. "We just, uh, had a little mishap with the sprinkling system."

He stared down at her, only a couple of feet between them. "I don't have a sprinkling system."

"I know that now." She kept her pretty eyes on his without flinching.

Something bubbled in his stomach and not until the laughter burst from his mouth did Owen realize what it was. She seemed to deflate before him, whether out of embarrassment or relief, he wasn't sure.

"So who's worse?" he asked once he quieted down. "Tar Baby or Marie?"

Natalie sucked in a breath. "At this point? Maybe Tar Baby."

Owen whistled through his teeth as he sidestepped Natalie, and his dog came outside with him. "Stay, Tar Baby." The dog sat and stayed.

"I don't know how you do that," she said.

"I'm the pack leader." He found Marie standing over the hose, rubbing her hands together in the chilly stream of water. "Marie, sweetheart," he called. "Come on in. You should get in the tub." He cast a long look at Natalie. "You can get on home and clean up, if you want." He spoke in a kind voice, glad it didn't sound like a command he might give to his boys or his dog.

"I think I can just use the kitchen sink," Natalie said. "I worked for an hour on the barbeque beef, and I'm starving."

Owen smiled, feeling the joy all the way to the bottom of his feet. "Great. I'll get Marie in the tub and take care of this rascal." He reached for Tar Baby and ruffled the dog's fur. "Stay," he commanded again as Marie approached.

"Hey, Uncle Owen." She beamed up at him. "Natalie taught me how to knead dough today."

Owen met Natalie's eye over Marie's head. She wore a look of apprehension tinged with pride. "She did, huh? That's great, sweetheart." He guided her toward the doorway. "What happened with the water?"

"Well, Tar Baby found a dead bird and he wouldn't stay away from it. So I grabbed the hose and sprayed him, like you said I should. And Natalie thought it would be a good idea to water that brown patch of lawn by the back fence. But the sprinklers don't work, and there was water everywhere!" She looked absolutely gleeful, and Owen chuckled.

He moved down the hall ahead of Marie and flipped on the bathroom light. "Where's the dead bird now?"

"Natalie wrapped it in paper and put it in the trashcan."

He couldn't imagine her doing anything of the sort. In high school, she'd made him kill the spiders, and while she'd gone hiking and fishing with him, she wouldn't go hunting and her one rule of fishing was that she didn't have to gut the catch.

"She did?"

"Yup." Marie pulled down a towel as he started the water in the tub. It ran cold for several seconds before getting warm. "She's awesome, Uncle Owen. I like her the best of all the nannies."

"Marie," he said in a warning voice. "I just had her come today. I have two more interviews this weekend." He pointed to the sink. "Put your muddy stuff in there. I'll wash it later tonight." He stepped out of the bathroom and pulled the door closed. He stared at it a moment, wondering if he should just cancel the other interviews.

Marie liked Natalie—and if Owen were being honest, he did too. He hadn't laughed like he had tonight in a long, long time.

He glanced down the hall, where he could hear the kitchen sink running. Moving on silent boots, he crept to the end of the hall and watched Natalie scrub the mud from her skin. He liked her presence in his home, liked the way she had fit right in, filled the holes in his life so easily, the way she always had.

Powerful fear pounded through him and he stepped

outside to spray down his dog. He ground his teeth together, his frustration coming as quick as his earlier exuberance. He didn't have time to get to know Natalie again. He needed to focus on Marie, on making sure she had everything she needed to thrive, be happy.

Maybe what she needs is Natalie, he thought, further fogging his thoughts. He wasn't sure what was right, what was wrong, what he should do. As he held Tar Baby with one hand and sprayed him with the other, he prayed for clarity of thought, hoping the Lord didn't mind a plea covered in a bit of mud.

———

Natalie combed through Marie's feather-fine hair, inhaling the clean scent of the little girl. "There you go, sweetheart," she said, adopting the term of endearment Owen always used for her. "Now go sit at the table. It's time to eat."

Marie jumped down from the counter and took a seat at the table. Owen had found a folding chair in the garage so there were three seats around his small table. Natalie had covered most of the surface with food: freshly made hamburger buns, barbeque beef, and coleslaw. She'd even made pink lemonade and coffee. Somewhere deep inside her, she hoped Owen would send Marie to bed and ask Natalie to stay for coffee. Maybe she could snuggle into his side on the couch while the now-clean dog lay at their feet.

The picture-perfect vision flew from her mind when Owen said, "Natalie, will you say grace?" He extended his hand toward her to take, and when she slid her fingers along his, every cell in her body flared to life. Things she'd forgotten about him, about their past together, crowded to the front of her mind. She'd always adored the way he cared for her, protected her, cherished her.

She lifted her eyes to his, her throat unable to let words pass. His expression stormed with emotion, and she couldn't name a single one. Maybe because he was cycling through them so fast. She wondered what her touch conjured for him, and perhaps foolishly, she hoped she'd find out. Soon.

She ducked her head. "Dear Lord," she began, thankful her voice had remembered how to work. When she finished the prayer, she squeezed Owen's hand before letting go and dishing up a scoop of coleslaw for Marie.

His house was warm, and the conversation was easy because Owen asked Marie questions and told her stories about the horses at the riding center where he worked. Once they finished, Owen told Marie to go get her homework so he could look at it, and the girl skipped down the hall.

"She's so great," Natalie said as she watched her go.

"She likes you too." Owen stacked plates and took them to the kitchen sink. "So, Natalie, tell me about yourself."

Her first reaction was to laugh, but she managed to turn it into a cough when she realized he wasn't joking. "You know me, Owen," she said, heat rising to her face at how well he'd known her. She took the leftover beef into the kitchen. "Do you have any plastic containers? I'll put this in the fridge."

He pointed to a cupboard on the bottom, near her left leg. She opened it and pulled out what she needed.

"I think you might have changed in the past twelve years," he said in that quiet, unnerving way he had. That simple voice that seemed to pierce through any defenses Natalie had been able to erect.

"I have," she said. "A little, at least." She twisted to put the leftovers in his fridge.

He scanned her from eyes to toes. "Oh, more than a little." A coy smile rode his lips and he glanced away quickly.

Was he checking her out? She goggled at him, suddenly self-conscious about how she looked. She'd always hated how her left eye squinted more than her right when she smiled. She thought her shoulders too boxy and her legs too long. She could never find jeans that didn't look like crops or capris.

"So what do you do with your day?" he asked, drawing her away from the petty things she didn't like about herself.

"I, well, I serve on the library board," she said. "But that's easy. A meeting every month and a few things to do. Nothing hard." She exhaled as she returned to the table for the buns. "I teach ballet at the studio over in the Historic District. And I teach cooking classes at the church. I'm doing a pie class in October and November for Thanksgiving."

"Hmm." He washed the dishes by hand though he had a

dishwasher. She wondered if it was broken or if he just liked the motion of cleaning. "Did you ever join a ballet company?"

Regret knifed through her. "No," she said. "I did graduate in dance and dance pedagogy, but I never auditioned for a company."

He turned back to her, his hands sudsy and soft. "Why not?"

She shrugged, glad when Marie came skipping back into the kitchen. "All done, Uncle Owen."

Owen didn't remove his gaze from Natalie's as he wiped his hands and reached for the little girl's homework. Then his eyes flitted across the page. "Looks good, sweetheart. What are we gonna do now?"

She looked at Natalie and back to her uncle. "Is Nat staying?"

Owen's eyebrows lifted. "Nat?" He switched his gaze back to hers. "I guess *Nat* can stay if she wants."

Marie turned her blue eyes, full of pleading, on Natalie. "Do you like movies? Owen has tons of movies."

"Oh, he does, huh?" Natalie reached for the girl's hand. "Which one is his favorite?" She let Marie lead her into the living room, where the girl knelt down and rifled through the cabinet in the entertainment center.

"This one." Marie held up a DVD case, and Natalie took it.

She couldn't help her laughter this time. "The Cowboys?" She glanced over her shoulder to where Owen leaned sexily in the doorway. "Seems about right. At least that hasn't changed about you."

He pushed away from the wall and joined them in the living room. "Not much has changed on my end," he said, but his voice held a false note.

"Sure," she said, nudging him with her shoulder. Flirting with him felt easy, natural, the way it always had. She was glad that hadn't changed either. "Same rugged face. Same five o'clock shadow. Same hat." She peered up at it. "Is that the *exact* same hat?"

He grinned at her, lighting her insides like he'd draped them in a string of Christmas lights. "Of course not."

"Looks the same."

"Looks can be deceiving," he said as he sat on the end of the couch and let Marie snuggle into his side.

Natalie took the spot on the other end of the couch, wishing she had Marie's spot but also scared of being in that position again. Or maybe she wasn't. She wasn't quite sure how to make sense of her tumultuous feelings.

Marie fell asleep about ten minutes into the movie, and Owen lifted the girl effortlessly into his strong arms and took her down the hall to her bedroom. When he returned, Natalie was pulling on her running shoes. "I should go."

"You never did like my westerns," he said, a playful edge to his words.

Feeling brave, and blessed, and bold, she said, "I like everything western. The men. The hats." She ticked the items off on her fingers. "The music. The simple life. The country." She moved toward the door. "I was never the one with the problem of staying in town, Owen."

"I know that." His words barely reached her ears and yet it sounded like he'd shouted. Sometimes she wished he would. Anything would be better than his strong steadiness.

"Natalie," he said in that blasted voice. "I have two more interviews, but I think I'm going to cancel them."

She locked eyes with him, hardly daring to hope. He watched her as he said, "Marie likes you, and she's everything to me right now. If she's happy, I'm happy. If she's not, I'm not."

Natalie wasn't quite sure what to say to that, so she stood by his front door, waiting for him to continue.

"I need to be at work by five-forty-five," he said. "That's AM, sweetheart, and I know you hate getting up early." He tipped his hat forward as he reached up and rubbed the back of his head. He settled his cowboy hat back into place. "I'd need you here at five-thirty so I can go. Marie doesn't need to be up until seven-thirty." He hooked his thumb over his shoulder, indicating the hallway.

"That's why she's so tired. I get her up and take her next door. But if you're here, she can sleep. You can too. I don't care. As long as she gets up and gets to school by eight-thirty. Then I need you to pick her up every afternoon. You don't have to make dinner, but if you want to, let me know what groceries to buy." He took a deep breath, and it might have been the most she'd ever heard Owen speak at once.

"Which reminds me," he said. "What do I owe you for dinner tonight?"

"Nothing," she choked out.

"I didn't have that roast in my fridge." He frowned. "I'll pay for the food."

"That's good to know." She flashed him a smile that left her lips too quickly.

"It's Friday tomorrow," he said. "Can you come in the morning? Pick her up from school? We can talk more about pay and grocery lists and stuff then."

"Sure thing, Owen."

His eyes closed in a long blink. "Thank you, Natalie."

She nodded and slipped out the front door. Her heart felt like dancing while at the same time it felt like she'd just tied it to a cement block and pushed it into the river. Who was she kidding? There was no way she could spend every evening with Owen Carr, every morning caring for his niece, and not fall in love with him again.

And that scared her more than anything ever had in her life.

———

The grass against Natalie's bare feet is cold and rough. She presses back a giggle as she crosses her backyard and ducks into the neighboring yard. Her heart feels like it might burst from a cage, the way birds explode from trees when spooked. It's Halloween, and icy, and after midnight, but Owen said he'd be waiting on the water tower. She's already been home, already washed the costume makeup from her face, already hugged her father good-night.

But Owen said he'd be waiting on the water tower, and so Nat goes. She steals across the blocks like a thief in the night, her dark clothing blending into the country sky.

The water tower sits on the northern edge of town, much closer to Owen's house than hers. He confessed to her last week that he often goes there to think, to write song lyrics, to get outside when it's too hard to think inside.

He said he's never told a girl about it, *she thought as the structure comes into view. His comment had made her wonder how many other girls he's been out with, but she already knew that answer. Everyone in Gold Valley seemed to know everyone else's business, especially in her high school class.*

And she knew Owen had only dated one other girl, and only for a few weeks. She wasn't sure why. He was gorgeous, thoughtful, talented. He makes her insides hum with a smile, her blood pound with the touch of his fingers to hers, her head swim when he mentions he wants to kiss her but he wants the moment to be right.

Please let this be the right moment, *she prays as she locates the ladder on the side of the water tower and starts up.*

"Hey," Owen whispers when she arrives on the platform. "You came." His smile dampens the light from the moon and he gestures her closer. She goes gladly, and not only because the temperature is dangerously close to freezing. "Why don't you have shoes?"

"I left them in the garage on accident." She snuggles into his warm side, tucking her feet between his legs. "What are you thinking about?"

"Just writing a song in my head." He'd said he sometimes brings his guitar with him, but the neighbors heard him playing

and reported it. *He claims to have barely made it into the trees before the cops showed up. He hasn't brought his guitar since.*

"Sing some of it for me?" *she asks, wishing she could freeze this moment with the two of them and hold onto it forever.*

"Nah," *he says.* "It's not ready yet." *His lips land lightly on her temple, and she turns into him. Their eyes meet, and she sees heat and desire and kindness and apprehension in his. She wonders if he's ever kissed a girl before.*

She hasn't kissed a boy yet, and desperation surges. She wants Owen to be her first kiss. Heck, she could end the sentence at she wants Owen.

The moment seems to stretch into the night, elongating until finally Owen closes his eyes and dips his head so his mouth meets hers.

She's still not sure if Owen's ever kissed a girl before, but he sure is an excellent kisser. Bright light paints the backs of her eyelids, and a rushing sound fills her ears, and she decides that kissing isn't so bad—as long as it's Owen's lips against hers.

He pulls back slightly, his hand cupping the side of her face, a warm shield against the chilly night. "Nat," *he whispers.* "You're somethin' special."

She grins, slides onto his lap, and kisses him again.

CHAPTER 4

*N*atalie jerked out of a sound sleep, the memory of that bright autumn moon, the rough planks of the water tower platform, and the lovely pressure of Owen's lips on hers rippling through her mind.

She hadn't thought about their first kiss—her first kiss ever—in many years. Now her fingers drifted to her lips, slid along her jaw. Owen was exceptionally skilled at making her feel cherished, loved, valued. He'd always included her in his thoughts, his worries, his plans. She'd never dreamed he'd leave town without a word the day after their high school graduation.

That wasn't the plan. The plan was to go to Nashville in the fall. The plan was to go to Nashville together. The plan was to go to Nashville after they'd gotten married.

He hadn't bought her a ring yet. He said his parents would freak out if he got engaged in high school. In fact, the day he left town, Natalie had been expecting a proposal not an empty room and silence.

Horrified at how easily the repressed memories surged through her, she flung her comforter off her legs and got out of bed. She crossed the hall and began her meditation pose, trying to clear her mind, trying to see through the fog of her dream, trying to understand what all of this meant.

Maybe it really is a second chance for us, she thought. The idea wouldn't easily leave her mind, though she reminded herself of Owen's intense job, his unyielding devotion to Marie, his haunted expression that said things had happened in his past he needed to overcome.

She went through her exercises, taking the whole thirty minutes to decompress, find her center, before returning to bed. The clock on her bedside table told her she'd have to get up in less than two hours to be ready and over to Owen's by five-thirty.

She laid back in bed, sure she'd never be able to fall asleep. But she did. And she dreamt again of Owen, a smile on her face at the beautiful memories they'd made together.

Later that morning, but still much too early for normal humans to be awake, Natalie parked in front of Owen's house. She didn't have to ring the doorbell or knock, because he sat on the front porch, his guitar across his lap. He wasn't playing, a fact that made her heart ache.

"You still play?" she asked, settling onto the stoop beside him.

"Yeah."

"Want to play me something?"

"It's too cold," he said. "Makes the strings flat."

It was an excuse if she'd ever heard one, but she let it slide. "Maybe later, then." She stifled a yawn, her mind circling that kiss she'd experienced as a seventeen-year-old.

"Sure, later." He stood and held open the screen door for her. "Marie's backpack is in her room. It's ready to go. I packed her lunch. It's in a brown bag in the fridge."

Natalie nodded, noting the low lamplight and how everything seemed to be in the exact same spot as when she'd left last night. Owen wasn't messy, but he didn't straighten up all the time either.

He crossed to the corner of the room by the television and set his guitar in its stand. She wanted to ask him about Nashville, and what had happened there, and why he didn't sign a second record deal. But he said, "Well, I best be off," and headed back out the front door.

Natalie employed all her self-control to keep from watching him stride down the sidewalk to his truck. No need to be obvious, she'd told herself on the short drive over.

With nothing to do, and another two hours to kill, she lay on the couch and pulled the same blanket she'd used last night onto her legs. After setting an alarm on her phone for seven-thirty, she drifted back to sleep, Owen's clear, crisp voice ringing in her ears, singing the song he'd written for her all those years ago.

Owen couldn't explain his bad mood. Maybe because he'd ended one day with Natalie as the last person he saw, and started the next with her as the first person he saw. He'd often dreamed of a life like that with her. A life where they were married, and raising a family, and sharing their deepest fears, ambitions, feelings, aspirations.

And this...this shell of that wasn't good for Owen. He'd lain awake last night until he'd managed to convince himself everything would work out. But seeing Natalie this morning before the sun had risen had rankled him.

He didn't do things halfway, and this new partnership with Natalie felt like halfway. Not all in, not all out. Tell her goodnight, welcome her in the morning. Let her take care of Marie, make dinner, watch movies. But then watch her disappear into the night. No, Owen didn't like that at all.

And that was the real problem.

"It's not gonna work," he muttered as he pulled into the parking lot at Silver Creek. He was glad he hadn't rushed himself to cancel the other two interviews. Not that he'd had much time. Natalie had stayed until almost nine o'clock, and that felt like midnight to Owen. He hadn't been able to do much more than kick off his boots and collapse on his bed, Tar Baby at his side.

He killed the engine in his truck but didn't get out. His boys didn't deserve his bad mood. Several of them came from less-than-ideal home situations, and had turned to gangs or drugs as a way to belong. Several of them had fathers who brought their bad moods home and took out their frustrations on their wives and children. Owen wouldn't do that to his boys.

"It's Friday," he told himself. "You have the next three days off. You don't need Natalie—or anyone—until Tuesday. It'll work out." These were the same things he'd told himself last night so he could sleep. He wasn't quite sure how it would work out, and he knew from past experience that things didn't just magically get better. Boots didn't put themselves away. Dishes didn't wash themselves because he was tired. Dinner didn't appear on the table just because he was hungry.

His frustration remained, but he shoved it down, down, down and went to get his boys up for the day.

By that afternoon, he'd managed to put Natalie on a shelf in his head. She stayed there while he did a riding lesson with a group of girls. The twelve-week program ended at the end of the month, and everyone at Silver Creek had gotten pretty good at working with a horse. His boys, especially, as they did it everyday.

"Owen," someone called, and he turned from the rail where he was watching a tiny fourteen-year-old maneuver a horse named Kimchi around a barrel. Dr. Richards was moving toward him, and Owen went to meet him.

"Trevor's father is here." Dr. Richards looked over Owen's shoulder. "Norah can handle the rest of the lesson, can't she?"

"She's gotten real good with the horses," Owen said. "Let me go tell my boys to come over and put them away when the girls are done. I'll grab Trevor while I'm there, and we'll be over to your office in a few minutes."

"I'll talk to Norah."

Owen watched the man tromp right through the dirt and hay in his shiny shoes, a smile forming deep in his gut. Owen loved working at Silver Creek, loved the people he worked with and called friends. They'd been there for him through Tasha's death, and it had only taken an hour to empty his cabin because so many counselors had come to help.

A rush of appreciation filled him and he tipped his chin toward the rafters in the barn. "Thank you," he murmured. A peaceful feeling floated down from the sky and wrapped itself around Owen, exactly what he needed to remember that the Lord loved him, was aware of him and his situation.

What do I do about Marie? he asked. When the earth didn't shake and a voice didn't rend the air, he turned to go get Trevor and talk to his boys about putting the horses away before they went to their sports class.

He delivered his message and collected Trevor and his backpack. "You excited?" he asked the boy as they walked to the main building.

"Nervous and excited," the sixteen-year-old said. "I haven't seen my father in three months."

Owen clapped his hand on Trevor's shoulder. "He wants to see you or he woudn't have come."

"He didn't get up to say good-bye to me." Trevor spoke so low, Owen could barely hear him. He dipped his head and trained his eyes on the sidewalk in front of him. "He didn't come for Parents' Day."

Owen paused, which made Trevor stop too. "Trevor, remember that you're not the only one dealing with your addictions. You're not the only one who's suffered." He didn't want to add to Trevor's anxiety and load, but part of the recovery process was learning that one's actions weren't isolated events—and Owen knew better than most. Sure, he hadn't gotten involved with dangerous substances or broken the law. But he had abandoned his family and broken hearts with a single decision. Trevor had essentially done the same.

"You think he really wants to be here?"

"I talked to him on the phone," Owen said. "He said he wanted to take you to the game. So yes, I think he wants to *see you.*" Owen started moving again. "C'mon. You can do hard things."

Trevor came with him, constantly adjusting the straps on his backpack. Owen understood the squirmy feeling. When he'd come crawling back to Gold Valley, he'd had to apologize to his parents and Tasha, who was married and had a one-year-old baby Owen had never met. The way they'd welcomed him with open arms had taught Owen a valuable lesson. Yes, they'd been hurt, badly even. But they still loved him. He'd done everything he could since then to make sure they knew he loved them too.

The one person he hadn't set things right with was Natalie, and all at once he realized what the Lord wanted him to do.

Make things right with her.

"There they are," Dr. Richards said. "Mister Keller, this is our groomsman and at-risk counselor, Owen Carr. I believe you spoke with him last week."

Owen pushed his personal problems and refreshing revelations to the back of his mind so he could focus. It was hard, because though Owen knew what he should do, he had no idea *how* to accomplish making things right with his high school sweetheart without hurting her again.

And he really didn't want to do that.

CHAPTER 5

*O*wen couldn't help his goofy grin as he went back to the horse barn to check on his boys. Trevor's father had been personable and kind and he'd hugged Trevor to his chest like the boy was a coveted prize.

Since caring for Marie full-time these last six months, Owen had developed tender, parental feelings he didn't understand. Watching that father and his boy had warmed Owen's heart and pricked his eyes with tears.

He was smiling because genuine happiness pranced through him. He entered the barn and knew immediately that something was wrong. His boots froze to the ground as he scanned the area.

His boys weren't brushing down horses and hanging saddles. No, they'd gathered at the far end of the aisle, near Blackjack's stall. The tall, black horse stood at the rail, his head draped over the top.

Owen hurried toward them, a dozen thoughts scattering through his mind. "Boys?" he called. "What's goin' on?"

The boys parted to reveal additional people in the barn. That shock of blonde hair…. "Marie?" Owen's heart pumped out an extra beat at the sight of his petite niece giggling as Blackjack's lips tickled her palm.

"Uncle Owen!" The girl launched herself at him and he swung her into his arms. "Nat brought me to see the horses."

"I can see that."

"I like that black one. One of them boys said maybe I could ride 'im."

Owen arrived at the group, his eyes traveling over the group. All five of his boys watched him with a slight edge of worry in their expressions. Natalie wore a look of pure panic, and her fingers gripped the rail next to Blackjack's head like she needed the fence to stay standing.

"Which one told you that?" Owen asked.

Marie pointed at Stanley, who shrugged one shoulder, a hopeful half-smile forming on his face.

"Well, I did leave Stanley in charge." He beamed at Marie. "So I guess you can ride 'im." He ran one hand down Blackjack's nose and gathered the strength and calm energy from the horse. "He needs a saddle."

"I'll get it, Mister Carr." Cory bolted down the aisle.

"You boys'll be late for your athletic activity." He scanned the remaining group. Sometimes he had extremely athletic boys, and sometimes he didn't. This group hadn't particularly enjoyed their physical education. "Should I radio over to Mister Barney and tell him you're going to ride horses today?"

Guy's face brightened, and two other boys said, "Yes, Mister Carr," in unison.

He almost flinched at the formality, wondered what Natalie thought of these boys being so military with him. "All right." He set Marie on her feet. "So we need eight horses."

"Oh, I'm not riding." The first words Natalie had said landed like bombs in Owen's ears. He loved the sweet timbre of her voice, always had. A corner of his heart seemed to melt on the spot, the first sign that he was in real trouble with the woman.

"Sure, you are," he said. "You brought Marie, and she wants to ride."

She shook her head, her long ponytail swishing back and forth. "I haven't ridden a horse since—" She swallowed and pressed one hand to her heart. "I'm not riding."

Disappointment cut through Owen. She'd ridden with him several times in high school. The last time, they'd taken the horses to Bear Mountain and gone horseback riding to a campsite only accessible down a narrow path. Was that the last time she'd been on a horse?

"All right," he said as Cory returned with a saddle and began preparing Blackjack. "You can go on home, if you want. I'll be done after this. Marie can stay with me." The girl had gravitated back to the horse, and Owen wondered why he'd never brought her to ride before. She obviously loved horses and they could heal unseen hurts. He knew better than most.

"Maybe I'll stay and watch."

"Might as well ride, then." They seemed locked in a silent battle, her hazely-gold eyes practically shooting fire. He turned away. "Boys, go get your gear. Guy, saddle Ole Red for me, will you?"

"Sure thing, Mister Carr."

"Cory, we're all ridin' instead of going to sports today."

The boy whooped. "Can I have Johnny Depp?"

"Better go claim 'im," Owen said. "Jesus likes him too."

Cory's eyes narrowed before he crouched down in front of Marie. "He's ready for ya, Marie."

She smiled at him. "Thank you."

Owen swore Cory's chest swelled to four times its normal size. He met Owen's eye, who nodded slightly, before hurrying back to the tack room. Owen picked up Marie and set her on his shoulders. "Well, let's ride this black one. His name's Blackjack." He opened the gate and moved into the stall with the horse. He set Marie in the saddle and then pulled out his radio to let Barney know his boys wouldn't be coming that day.

With that done, he collected the reins in his hand and started toward the outdoor arena. He startled when he realized Natalie had joined him in the stall. It barely seemed big enough for the both of them, as well as the horse. Her fingers brushed against his, and he jerked back.

"Mister Carr, huh?" She kept her face toward the ground, but he heard the smirk in her voice.

He grunted and stepped toward the back of the stall. He led the horse and Marie out into the waning sunshine, and Natalie followed. She went to the side and settled on the top fence rung to watch. He couldn't help watching her, drinking in the length of her legs in the dark jeans she wore, imagining what it would be like to slide his hands up her sides in that navy polka-dot sweater, remembering the silky quality of that hair.

He cleared his throat and focused on Marie instead. Marie was safe. Marie needed him. Marie didn't cause three years of memories to churn and collate in his poor, over-worked mind.

With every step around the arena, a new idea for how he could make things right with Natalie flitted in and then out of his brain. By the time Guy arrived with Ole Red, Owen couldn't have been more grateful he didn't have to use his energy to walk. Thinkin' about Natalie took everything he had, and with her so physically close, he couldn't force her from his mind.

———

Natalie perched on the fence, new feelings of awe and pride and adoration and peace rising through her. Everything Owen did, everything he said, she found attractive. Something connected the two of them, no matter how much she wished it wouldn't. Or maybe she didn't wish that.

The majestic way he held himself in the saddle reminded her of his athleticism. The quiet way he commanded his boys and they obeyed testified of their love for him. The softness in his eyes when it came to Marie told her that he'd meant exactly what he'd said. If the girl was happy, Owen was too. And Natalie wanted Owen to be happy.

She'd seen the sadness in his eyes, the absolute pain, the terrifying worry. She wanted to erase all of it, ease his mind, help if she could. If she were being honest with herself, she also wanted answers. Answers to why he'd left early. Answers to why he didn't come back for her. Answers to why he'd come home when he'd seemingly done well in the country music business.

Owen watched her a lot too, almost like a magnetic force drew his gaze to her position on the fence. She pretended not to notice, but she felt his presence so strongly, she knew the moment he glanced her way.

When he called an end to the riding, she pulled out her phone and sent a text to the pizza joint in town. She could swing by there and pick up dinner on the way home since she hadn't had time to make anything.

A sick feeling rose through her when she saw the two missed calls. The number was familiar—it was the loan company for her car. She hadn't paid the bill in three months, and she couldn't swallow past the lump in her throat.

"Everything okay?" Owen's question jolted her and she almost dropped her phone.

"Fine." She stuffed the phone in her back pocket. "I ordered pizza for dinner from Luigi's. Want me to stop by and pick it up?"

"I can do it," he said. "Then I can pay for it."

She pressed her lips together and nodded. "Okay then. I'll see you later."

His hand landed on her arm and even through the sweater she wore, his touch burned. His touch ignited a fire in her stomach so hot she sucked in a breath to cool it.

"You're coming over, right?" he asked, his navy eyes penetrating all her pretended defenses.

"I think—I think I'll get on home."

"Natalie, we need to talk."

About what? she wanted to rage at him, suddenly angry that he could be so calm while touching her. Did she not affect him at all anymore? Why did she have to deal with strong desires, with old hurts, with spiraling emotions, and he didn't? Had he really dismissed her that easily?

"I don't have to work again until Tuesday," he said. "But I'd like you to come spend some time with Marie tomorrow."

"We can talk then," she said, adjusting her baking plans in her mind.

His eyebrows pinched together and his hand fell from her arm. "Don't you want dinner?"

She did. Oh, she did. She wanted to eat everything in sight to soothe the seeping wounds in her heart. But she didn't want to do that in front of Owen. "I can—" The air left her lungs as Marie flung her arms around Natalie's waist and hugged her tight.

"Thank you, Nat. The horses were awesome, just like you said they'd be."

She stroked the girl's soft hair and smiled down at her. "You're welcome, sweetheart." She unwound the child's hands and knelt in front of her. "I'll see you later, okay? Your uncle says I can come tomorrow." She tucked Marie's hair behind her ear and leaned closer. "I ordered your favorite pizza: olives and cheese. Don't let him eat it all." She grinned as Marie looked up at Owen.

"I won't, Nat." She cocked her head to the side. "You aren't gonna come eat with us?"

Natalie didn't know what to say. She stood and brushed the dirt from her jeans, searching for the right thing to tell Marie.

"Please come," Owen said.

Fireworks popped through Natalie at the soft insistence in his voice. She'd heard it before, when he'd invited her to the water tower, when his dog had gotten sick and he'd needed a comforting shoulder to lean on. She'd never seen Owen Carr cry. The man was too powerful, too stoic, for that. But he did possess a surprisingly soft side, and she'd adored that about him from the moment she'd started dating him.

"Mister Carr, all the horses are away for the night."

"Thank you, Stanley." Owen didn't look away from Natalie. "Remind the boys I'll be gone until Tuesday, and I want a good report from Trenton when I return." He cut a glance at Stanley.

"Have a good weekend, Owen." The boy started toward the barn's exit.

"You too, Stanley." Owen fixed his gaze back on Natalie. "So, whaddya say? You gonna come eat pizza with us?"

A grin burst onto her face, though her insides felt a bit wobbly. "Oh, all right. But I have to get home early. I have a lot of baking to do."

"Baking?" Owen latched his hand onto Marie's as they walked.

"Yeah, I'm prepping for my pie class at the church. Remember I told you about that?"

"Maybe you need some taste-testers," he suggested.

She laughed into the sky, and it felt good. "You always were a sucker for sweets."

"I'm just tryin' to help a pretty lady out."

Her feet froze to the ground, but Owen and Marie kept moving. "C'mon," he called back to her like he hadn't said anything out of the ordinary. But that hum had started in her core again, and she knew if she went to Owen's for dinner tonight, there would be no going back.

CHAPTER 6

*N*atalie sat in her car on the street outside Owen's house. His truck had been in the driveway when she'd arrived fifteen minutes ago. She couldn't get herself to go inside, though she desperately wanted to.

Because she also wasn't sure she should. Her old feelings for Owen had faded over time. Softened. Buried themselves deep. But they hadn't disappeared. Every minute she spent with him, she liked him a little bit more. Every thought she had of being with him again brought excitement mixed with terror.

Her phone rang and she fumbled for it on the passenger seat next to her. Of course it was Owen. The man was as relentless as he was handsome. She let the phone ring and ring. When it fell silent, she put the call volume on vibrate and left the phone in her console. She stepped from the car and smoothed down her sweater.

She'd been warring with herself all day. Warring about what she should do when it came to Owen. Leap in with wild abandon? Or take it one step at a time, carefully, cautiously easing into a relationship with him?

The fact that she was even considering a relationship with a man was hard for her to stomach. She valued her freedom above all else, and the man had a child now. They wouldn't be jetting off to exotic destinations or living a country music star lifestyle, as she'd once dreamed. No, everything had changed—*she'd* changed—and she wasn't sure her future included a husband or a family.

She knocked on the front door, and immediate boot-steps sounded against the wood floor on the other side. Owen flung open the door and stared at her. "Thought you weren't comin'."

"I came." She reached for the screen door handle. She had no excuse for her tardiness, so she didn't offer one. "I hope you saved me something to eat."

"You ordered three pizzas." He stepped back to let her in. "And cheese bread. So yeah, there's plenty to eat."

She gave him a sultry smile. "I remember you eating a whole pie yourself, Mister."

"I'm not saying I didn't." He followed her into the dining room, where he had all three pizzas on the table, along with a stack of paper plates. "I'm just saying there's still plenty to eat."

"Where's Marie?"

"In the tub." He sat at the table, the grease stains on his

plate saying he'd already eaten too. "You're late." He glanced up at her and gestured for her to sit down.

She obeyed and pulled a plate off the top of the stack. "I don't know what to do about you." She reached for a gooey piece of Hawaiian pizza. "So yeah, I was late, because I was sitting in my car on the curb, trying to figure things out." She gave him a glare, glad when he looked confused. "Happy now?"

"No," he barked.

"That makes two of us," she grumbled before she bit into her pizza, more confused than ever.

He exhaled like she was being difficult on purpose. "I—"

She glanced at him while she chewed, this perplexed side of Owen new. "You what?"

"I don't know what to do about you either." He twisted and reached behind him to the kitchen counter. When he faced her again, he placed a folder in front of him. "I had Doctor Richards help me draw up this agreement. It lays out what you'll get paid, the hours, the expectations." He cleared his throat. "All of that. You should read over it and see if you have any questions." He slid the folder toward her, but it went two inches before knocking into a pizza box.

She collected it, her face burning from her outburst. And his. Was this what their relationship would be like from now on? Each of them dancing around the other, frustrated and confused?

"Did you get the soda?" she asked after she swallowed her last bite.

"Right here." He stood, his chair scraping on the floor, and got the two-liter bottle. "You want ice?"

"Yes, please."

He muttered something that sounded dangerously like, "Of course she does," as he moved fully into the kitchen and opened the freezer.

Natalie ignored him. *She* wasn't the one who'd left town without warning. She flipped open the folder and started at the top of the first page. She'd work four hours in the morning, and three each afternoon. One hour in the morning would be dedicated to housework; one in the evening to cooking. He'd provide all cleaning supplies and groceries.

She'd be done by six o'clock each evening—plenty of time to do the pie classes at the church. And she had from nine-thirty to three o'clock open each day.

He set a glass of fizzing soda on the table in front of her, and she reached for it. When she saw the pay, she nearly knocked the glass over. She choked as she said, "Three thousand dollars a month?" She half-stood as she searched for his eyes.

He leaned against the kitchen sink, his arms folded across his impressive chest, his head tilted toward the floor. She couldn't read his face, and he didn't speak, and her heart spun spun spun.

"Owen, that's way too much."

"You don't like to get up early."

"So what?" She leaned into her palm on top of the paperwork. "That's like, twenty dollars an hour to babysit."

"I know how much it is. Marie is important to me. Who

THE COWBOY AND THE NANNY

takes care of her is important to me."

She wished he'd say, *You, Natalie, are important to me.*

He didn't.

"You can't be making that much at Silver Creek."

"You have no idea what I make at Silver Creek."

No, she didn't. But three thousand dollars a month just for his nanny? That didn't include his mortgage, his truck, gas, groceries, nothing else.

"I have to take her to the dance studio on Mondays and Tuesdays."

"I have every other Monday off. Otherwise, that's fine."

"Dinner will be late on those days."

He straightened, his presence filling the house, nearly knocking her over. "Do you not want the job? The money?"

"Of course I want it," she said. "I just—it's too much."

"What do you think is fair?"

"She's an eight-year-old girl. She can do a lot for herself."

"I don't want her to do anything for herself." He took a step forward. "She's…struggling. I want everything to be as easy as possible for her."

"Two thousand," she said. She could pay the rent on her house, pay what she owed on her car, and have enough to live on with that. "Not another penny more."

He shook his head. "I can't believe you—"

"Three thousand is too much." She picked up the folder and slapped it closed, stalking toward him. "Two thousand, or I'm not taking the job." She smacked the folder against his chest, standing toe-to-toe with him. She could see his dark eyes now, as close as she stood. Smell his subtle cologne too, and it nearly undid her frustration. He glared; she gave his attitude right back.

In the end, she softened first, sighing and letting her hand holding the folder drop to her side. "Two thousand dollars a month."

"Fine."

Down the hall, the tub started gurgling, signaling that Marie was finished with her bath. Natalie should stay to see her so Marie didn't think she hadn't come at all. "Fine," she echoed. Without thinking, and before she could talk herself out of it, she stretched up on her toes and ducked her face under the brim of Owen's hat. She swept her lips across his cheek and fell back as sparks erupted in her face.

"Thank you, Owen." She ducked her head so her hair would fall as a curtain between them, then scampered down the hall with the whispered excuse that she should see if Marie needed any help.

But instead of knocking on the girl's bedroom door, she hid around the corner and pressed her back into wall as she tried to even her ragged breathing. She couldn't believe she'd just kissed Owen Carr. A smile spread across her face and a giggle escaped her lips.

———

You missed.

The words rebounded from one side of Owen's skull to the other. *You missed.* What he'd wanted to say to her as she practically ran down the hall away from him.

You missed. My mouth is over here.

He sat on the couch now, the TV dark, and his fantasies spiraling completely out of control. He licked his lips, the desire to kiss Natalie—not on the cheek—almost overwhelming.

Finally, Marie joined him in the living room, a tablet in her hand. "Look, Uncle Owen. Natalie braided my hair."

Owen took in the intricate design in her hair. "It's real pretty, Marie."

"She said we could do a puzzle tomorrow." She sat on the couch next to him and turned on the tablet.

Irritation sang through him even though he'd suggested Natalie come spend some time with Marie tomorrow. "Sweetheart," he said. "I have the day off, remember?"

Marie looked up at him. "She can still come do a puzzle with me."

"Actually, I was thinking about going hiking. Maybe up to the waterfalls and then up to that picnic spot you like." He smiled, hoping she'd choose hiking over a puzzle. He loved spending time outside, and as the weather worsened, so did Owen's mood.

Marie scooted back into the couch and focused on her game. "Maybe she can come with us."

"No," Owen said at the same time Natalie did. She avoided Owen's eyes as she moved to Marie's side.

"I have to go, okay? I'll see you next week."

Marie threw her arms around Natalie's neck and gave her a sweet kiss on the cheek. Owen watched the exchange, his heart squeezing at the adoration in Natalie's eyes, at the way she squeezed them closed as she squeezed Marie in return. In fact, his heart nearly melted right out of his chest, causing him to leap away from the couch and step toward the door.

Unfortunately—or fortunately, he wasn't sure—Natalie joined him a moment later. She glanced back to where Marie sat, absorbed in her device, and then to him. "See you Tuesday."

"Look," he said, reaching back to rub his neck. "I did say I wanted you to spend some more time with Marie. You can come with us tomorrow, if you want."

She considered him with a blank expression. "Where are you going?"

"I, uh, showed Marie that place you and I used to hike to. Past the clearing, up toward the rocks. There's a pool there in the spring, and she liked that." He could remember plenty of things he liked about that particular spot, only one of which was the way he'd kissed Natalie against those rocks.

She inched closer and the tether that had always existed between them electrified. "You took another girl to our special place?" A grin accompanied the words.

"She's nothing like you," he said, his voice turning husky. His fingers itched to reach out and pull her closer. He fisted them instead. "So much younger. A little cuter."

Natalie scoffed. "She's cuter than me?"

"You're not cute." His hand darted out against his will, sweeping along Natalie's hip and drawing her closer to him. "You're gorgeous."

"Owen," she said, falling back. "I still don't know what to

do about you."

"I need to make things right between us," he said. "I know that, and I want to. I just don't know *how*." He'd never felt so frustrated before, not even when he'd lost his record contract because of something someone else had done.

And then Natalie's fingers slipped between his and tightened. "You don't owe me anything."

"Sure, I do," he said. "I've already apologized, but—" He couldn't even bring himself to mention that he owed her so much more, and that the explanation he needed to give her didn't actually exist. At least he didn't know where to find it.

She glanced back to Marie, dropped his hand, and returned to the girl. "Marie, I'm gonna talk to your uncle outside for a second, okay?"

"Okay."

Natalie swept back into his personal space, reclaimed his hand, and towed him out the front door with her. He liked this in-charge version of Natalie, always had. He loved the feel of her hand in his. He enjoyed the scent of her skin, her hair, as he followed her to the front steps.

She sat and hugged her knees to her chest. "I'll admit that I'd like some answers."

Of course she would. And Owen wanted to give them to her. "You deserve them." He hung his head. "It's why I wanted to pay you three thousand dollars a month."

She sucked in a breath. "I don't need your money. I just need—" She cut off the words, and he was really interested in hearing the end of that sentence.

He tucked his hand through her elbow. "Will you come

tomorrow, Nat? We're not leaving until 'bout ten."

She sighed and leaned her head on his bicep the way she had so many times before. "I'll come, but only because Marie wants me to. And because I love hiking. And because when I ask you a question tomorrow, you'll answer it honestly." She tilted her head back to look at him. "Deal?"

Though his throat felt like he'd swallowed sawdust, he nodded. "Deal." He leaned down and pressed a kiss to her forehead, causing that sizzling sensation to zip along his skin.

She stood and had taken a few steps toward her car when she said, "You missed, you know."

"Missed?" he called after her, willing the darkness not to swallow her quite yet.

"Yeah." She stopped and twisted back toward him. "My mouth is a lot lower than that." The porch light glinted in her eyes and she laughed as she bounded across the lawn and got into her car.

He shook his head, warmth filling all the icy places inside his body. He'd been cold for so long and hadn't even realized it. Until now. Until Natalie. Until she came along and reminded him what it was like to live, to actually feel something but regret. He felt like a weight had been lifted from his shoulders, and not just because he had someone he could trust to take care of Marie. But because he had the possibility to make things right between the girl he'd loved once.

And could love again, he thought as he switched on the TV and Marie curled into his side.

CHAPTER 7

*O*wen woke at five a.m. like he usually did, despite not having to go to Silver Creek that morning. No matter how late he stayed up, his eyes popped open at five.

And he'd been up late last night, because after he'd thought he could fall in love with Natalie again, he'd realized how foolish and irresponsible he was being. He wasn't interested in repeating his mistakes with her. Didn't want to put his heart through that meat grinder again.

And Marie? Marie didn't need a new mother. No one—not even Natalie—could replace Tasha.

No, Owen just needed help with Marie. He didn't need a girlfriend, and Marie didn't need a new mom.

He heaved himself out of bed and into the shower. When he got out, he thought the air felt a bit chillier than normal. He checked the thermostat, bumped it up a little to get the furnace to come on, got dressed, and noticed that the furnace was blowing cold air.

Dread settled into his stomach. He hadn't had time to service the furnace yet, and it wasn't what he wanted to spend his Saturday morning doing. But Marie wasn't up yet, and he really didn't have anything else to do—unless sipping coffee and reading the Internet headlines counted.

He let Tar Baby out into the backyard and started a pot of coffee before hauling the ladder in from the shed. He plugged in the space heater and put it down the hall near the bedrooms so Marie wouldn't be too cold, then he climbed into his old attic and got to work.

An hour later, he'd replaced the filter and looked up how to change the flame sensor. He sat in the living room, directly under the vent blowing hot air into his house, feeling more accomplished than he had in a long time.

With a new plan in place to keep his distance from Natalie, he got his cup of coffee, queued up his laptop, and chuckled when Tar Baby curled into a ball on Owen's feet. He managed to live for an hour without the reminder that his sister had died and left him to take care of Marie. An hour where he didn't fret constantly about his high school sweetheart. An hour where his five years in Nashville didn't plague him.

All too soon, Marie woke and Owen's day started. He packed lunches and warm weather gear, all while teaching Marie what she should take with her when she went into the Montana wilderness. By nine-thirty, he had everything in the back of his truck, including the dog. Natalie hadn't signed the paperwork the previous evening, so he'd tossed it onto the seat, intending to get over to her place to get her signature and deliver the money he owed her for groceries.

Sometimes it really benefitted him to know everyone in town. Bryan, the grocer, had looked up her receipt, and he simply called the power company to find out her address. He pulled in front of the little white house twenty minutes before ten and decided to give her a few minutes.

He pulled out his phone and said, "Well, we're a little early. Should we call Grandma?"

Marie's face lit up. "Yes!"

He chuckled as he dialed his mother, knowing she'd probably been up at dawn to finish harvesting her garden. She answered after only one ring, and he said, "Hello, Ma. Got a pretty little lady who wants to talk to you." He passed the phone to Marie and leaned back against the seat with his eyes closed.

He jerked forward, his knee crashing into the dashboard when he heard Marie say, "Uncle Owen hired this nice lady to watch me." He whipped his head in her direction, but Marie didn't seem to notice a problem. "Yeah, she's real fun. Real pretty. I don't have to get up so early anymore."

Owen's heartbeat settled back to normal as Marie moved on to how Tar Baby had dug up the backyard after the sprinkler mishap. Marie finished, said, "I love you, Grandma," and handed the phone back to Owen.

He groaned silently as he imagined the questions his mother would ask about the nanny. Sure enough, she said, "So who did you hire to watch Marie?"

"An old friend," he said evasively, like that would work.

His mother tsk'ed. "Someone I know then."

"Ma, you know everyone in town." He suddenly felt too tired, and he hadn't even called Marie's other grandparents yet. At least they didn't know about Natalie. "It's Natalie Lower," he said, unwilling to play the charade any longer.

The silence on the other end of the line said it all. "I know, Ma, okay? I know. But she's great with Marie, and they get along great, and—" He turned toward the window so Marie wouldn't overhear. "She seemed like she needed the money." That last part hurt him to say, but say it he did. He wasn't sure why he felt that way, but he was exceptionally good at reading people, something that came in handy with the boys at Silver Creek.

"Have you talked to her yet?"

"I've spoken to her several times, Mom. I didn't just hire her out of nowhere."

"Owen."

"No, Ma. We're goin' hiking this morning. I'm hoping to get some things out in the open then."

You are, he told himself while at the same time he didn't want to have that conversation ever. He didn't want to admit to his fear, to the irrational feelings of being trapped, of not being able to fulfill his lifelong dream of going to Nashville if he waited. He still believed he'd made the right decision—*look at Natalie*, he thought. *She never auditioned for the ballet company.*

"I need to go," he said. "We'll see you at church tomorrow, okay?" He hung up with his mom and dialed Marie's father's parents. He did his best to keep them looped in to

Marie's life. They were even older than his parents, Tasha's husband Henry the youngest of five children. They lived in Idaho Falls, and they too answered after only one ring.

"Owen," Carol said. "How are you?"

"Doin' just fine, ma'am. Marie wanted to call this mornin'." He glanced at the girl and she set aside her tablet in favor of his phone. She told her other grandma all the same things as Natalie started backing out of her garage.

Owen motioned toward her and Marie nodded, so he got out of the truck and went to talk to her. She rolled down her window and peered up at him. "Hey," he said. "We were early so we thought we'd save you the drive over." He hooked his thumb toward the truck. "You can just throw your stuff in the back of the truck, and we'll go."

She opened the door and stepped out of the car, causing him to fall back a few paces. "How do you know where I live?"

"It's a small town, Nat." He didn't want to tell her of his investigative techniques.

She glanced toward the house like she was embarrassed of it. When she didn't say anything, he said, "Are you ready? What can I get for you?"

"Is it true that you were engaged when you lived in Nashville?" Her gaze swung back to his, and he felt like everything moved in slow motion. It took an hour to take a breath. A day for him to lift his hand to the back of his neck. He'd rub a rash onto the skin if he didn't stop with the nervous action.

"Yes," he managed to say.

"Did you get married?"

"No."

She cocked her head and frowned. "Are you going to give me more than one word answers today?"

"If you need them."

She folded her arms and settled her weight onto her back leg. "I need them."

"Yes, I was engaged. She was my manager. It was a mistake to mix business with pleasure, and things went south, and...." His voice dried up, the same way his heart had when Clarissa had botched his second deal and then broke up with him when he questioned her about it.

Natalie waited, those beautiful eyes filled with compassion. "And you broke up," she finished for him.

"She still has the ring. Wouldn't give it back."

Natalie gasped, her hand fluttering to her throat. "Wow."

"Yeah." He exhaled and looked toward Marie in the truck. She still held the phone to her ear. "I sure know how to pick 'em, don't I?"

She bent into her car and turned off the ignition. When she emerged, she held a paper plate of something that looked and smelled like chocolate.

"Are those brownies?" His mouth watered.

"I said I had some baking to do." She closed the door, stepped closer to him, and extended the treats toward him. "And I don't know about how you pick women," she said. "But I thought we were really good together." She didn't give him a chance to respond before turning back to the car and gathering her pack from the backseat. She handed it to him with challenge in her eyes. "Didn't you?"

"Natalie," he started. "I—I don't want to mix business with pleasure again."

She blinked at him, the realization coming slowly into those gold-flecked eyes. A blush crept into her face and she turned away quickly. "Of course not."

"I like you." His voice rang with the lie. He didn't just like her. He'd always *liked* her. He'd loved her once, and he thought he probably still did. "Marie adores you. But—" A gust of wind stole the lame explanation and she held up her hand to silence him anyway.

"I don't need you to explain," she said.

"I want to."

She shook her head and pressed her lips together. "Please don't."

"It's just that Marie just lost both of her parents, and we're still figuring out how we go together, and I don't—" He cleared his throat as she strode away from him, from his explanation. She pulled open the truck's door and climbed in with Marie.

Owen stared after her, stunned she'd walked away from him while he was in the middle of a sentence. She'd never done that before.

"No," he muttered. "You're the one who's great at leaving without an explanation." He followed her, threw her backpack into the bed of his truck, and took a deep breath. *She'd* said she'd wanted answers. *Guess she didn't like what she heard.*

79

He needed the peace and quiet of the Montana wilderness. Hopefully he'd be able to find the right words, give her the right answers, on their hike. He felt on the wrong side of the universe from her. The space between them felt insurmountable, and his heart cried as if alone and wounded in the wilderness.

He turned his thoughts to the Lord, and prayed for guidance, and strength, and clarity of thought so he wouldn't say anything to hurt Natalie further. She didn't deserve that. She deserved to be happy.

So do you. The words came into his mind as if spoken from the atmosphere. He took another breath and braced himself for a hard day.

———

The memories streaming through Natalie's head couldn't be contained. She smelled things she hadn't thought of in years. The fact that Owen didn't deviate from his favored brands of coffee and toothpaste and cologne didn't help. Not only that, but the fresh scent of the pine trees on this particular trail.

When they arrived at the pool, it was dry. The way Owen had tackled her there one spring, shocked her with that cold water, and then spent the afternoon warming her with his kisses paraded through her mind's eye as if it had happened yesterday.

She swallowed and turned away. She shouldn't have come on this hike, despite her love of the outdoors. Every step hurt, because she heard Owen tell her over and over again that he wasn't interested in her.

That's not what he said, she told herself with every other step, but she didn't quite believe herself. Despite holding her hand last night, despite the river of desire she saw in his eyes, despite inviting her on this excursion with a *please come*, he wasn't interested.

"C'mon, Marie," Owen said. "Here's your lunch."

Natalie turned away from the gorgeous scenery before her, the bright blue sky that usually calmed her, the green and red and orange trees. She found a rock several feet from where Marie had settled on the ground and pulled her pack off her back. Her shoulders finally relaxed and her leg muscles popped and tingled now that she'd stopped pushing them uphill.

Owen came over to her and sat immediately next to her. "It's nice up here. Jacket weather, but nice."

She took a long drink from her water bottle and simply nodded. She'd gotten answers to a couple of her questions just by asking one. She wasn't sure she wanted to know why he'd left four months before they'd talked about, why he hadn't married her first. With a jolt of clarity, she realized the answer would be the same one she'd gotten this morning.

He didn't want her. Wasn't interested.

She'd never thought Owen was a coward, but now thinking back, she realized he'd left town because he was afraid of telling her he wasn't interested. At least he hadn't done it again now.

"Natalie," he said, his gaze out on the splendid horizon before them. "I'm kind of a mess right now. I'm sorry about that."

"It's not your fault."

"I don't want to hurt you."

"You haven't."

He scoffed, turning the sound into a half-hearted chuckle. "I have eyes, Nat, and I can see you in a way not a lot of people can."

She busied herself by pulling out her lunch so she wouldn't have to verbally acknowledge the truth in his words. The thought of swallowing the brownies—German chocolate, Owen's favorite—made her sick.

"So everything I said this morning is going to make no sense when you hear what I'm going to say next."

"Maybe don't say it then." She unwrapped her granola bar and took a bite, the oats and honey making her stomach writhe. Or maybe that was the maddening man next to her.

"I want to say it." He sure took his time for something he wanted to do. She supposed he always had. He finally turned his body toward her, the weight of his stare an uncomfortable sensation after only two seconds.

"I want to go out with you."

She'd been planning to stare at a fallen branch ten yards away until he got up and left, but she couldn't help it when her head jerked toward his. She met his eyes, saw the sincerity in them.

"You're right," she said calmly, proud of herself for chan-neling her inner-Owen. "That makes no sense."

"I know it doesn't, but it's the only thing I've been able to think about since we left your place this morning."

"You should focus on building a safe place for Marie."

He shook his head and dropped his gaze to the sandwich he still hadn't bitten into. "Will you go out with me?"

"No."

He nodded, and nodded, and nodded. "All right." He got up and took his pack and lunch closer to Marie. They spoke in quiet tones and Natalie didn't know what they said. Everything in her wanted to call Owen back over, withdraw her rejection, go anywhere with him.

Well, most everything inside her. There was a spot right in the middle of her heart that cheered at her negative response. That reminded her she was better off alone, because then she could determine her happiness.

But she wouldn't ever be whole, and she knew it.

CHAPTER 8

Natalie saw Owen and Marie at church, but she didn't go over and say hello. She sat by her parents and she went over to Stephanie's in the evening. Another teacher at the studio, Stephanie held a Sunday dinner party for friends every week. Natalie's job was to supply the vegetable tray, something she did gladly.

When she arrived, she set the relish tray on the kitchen counter and sighed onto a barstool. "Rough week?" Stephanie asked. "Tell me about it before anyone else shows up." Stephanie had a quick smile, and straight teeth, and the curliest hair Natalie had ever seen. She was also loyal and kind, and if Natalie had to name her best friend, it would be Stephanie.

"I got the nanny job."

Stephanie paused in the stirring of her famous corn and bacon dip. "That's great, sweetie. Why do you look like someone ran over your cat?"

"The job's with Owen Carr."

Stephanie stared, her mouth turning into an O. "Your ex-boyfriend Owen Carr?"

"The one and the same." She buried her head in her hands. "What am I going to do?"

Stephanie abandoned her prep work and came around the counter to sit by Natalie. "You need the job, right?"

"More than you know." A nest of snakes struck in her stomach simultaneously. She really did need the money.

"Then take it. Just do the work. You'll hardly see him, right?"

Natalie didn't tell her about the meals she'd enjoyed for several nights in a row. She didn't have to stay for dinner. She wasn't getting paid to stay past six o'clock. "Right."

A timer went off, and Stephanie jumped up to check the lasagna bubbling in the oven. Dissatisfied by something, she pushed the tray back in and set the timer for ten more minutes. "Do you like the little girl?"

"She's wonderful. I'll be bringing her to the studio on Tuesday. You'll get to meet her."

"She's the one whose parents were killed in that car accident, right?"

"Right."

"So sad." Steph shook her head. "So here's a question: Why don't you want to work with Owen? From what you've said, you were in love with him."

She nodded. She had been in love with him. "He's in a tough spot right now," she said. "Not looking for a girlfriend." Which made his invitation to go out downright confusing. "Trying to figure out how to be a dad to an eight-year-old."

"Well, you can help him with that. You're so good with kids."

"He doesn't want my help."

"He obviously does, or he wouldn't have hired you." She smacked Natalie playfully with the back of a wooden spoon. Someone knocked on the door and voices entered the house.

"Jason and Bea are here," Natalie said, leaning back and catching sight of the couple. "Don't say anything. They grew up with Owen."

"Lips are sealed," Steph said, glancing toward the foyer to see how close the others were before leaning over the island. "But if you ask me, you should push the girlfriend issue. It's obvious you still like him." She straightened and said, "Hey, you two. Are those mint brownies?"

Natalie joined the conversation, laughed with her friends, felt loved and included. But in the back of her mind lingered Owen and his brooding, navy eyes that wouldn't release her.

Maybe she should do what Steph had suggested and push the girlfriend issue. See what Owen did. It was better than her plan to suffer alone in silence, avoiding him if at all possible, and crying herself to sleep at night. Not that she'd really do that—last night didn't count.

After a delicious dinner and great conversation, as Natalie rode the high of being with people she cared about, she dialed Owen. He didn't pick up, and she cursed herself for the after-ten-o'clock phone call. She hung up quickly and waited until she'd pulled all the way into her garage and had put the car in park.

Then she sent him a daring text.

I'd love to go out with you. Call me tomorrow and we can schedule something.

She immediately silenced her phone and entered the house with a small smile riding her lips. She plugged in her phone in the kitchen and set it face-down on the counter. She didn't want to know his response until she'd gotten a good night's rest.

And this time, she fell asleep without a single tear, but the hope ballooning in her chest was almost as difficult to deal with.

———

Owen endured Sunday as best as he could. He was up early, as usual, but he left late for church so he wouldn't have time to talk to his mother before the service began. He couldn't face her questions, mostly because he had no idea how to answer them.

He felt like a yo-yo, his emotions constantly jerking up and being thrown down. First, he was telling Natalie he didn't want to mix business with pleasure, and then he was asking her out. He didn't blame her for being confused, for rejecting him.

He just didn't know how to explain himself. He didn't want to mix business with pleasure, but that didn't mean he wasn't interested in her. But he hadn't said that, and he realized that what he had said had implied as much.

He stared into the darkness on Monday morning, wishing he could erase this weekend from his life. Yeah, he'd definitely made things worse with Natalie. When the pastor had announced that the fall class sign-ups were almost full, Owen had decided to register for her pie class.

After the service, he'd taken Marie to the tables by the classrooms, where he found classes from sewing to chess to cooking. Natalie's pie class was by far the most popular, and he saw she was teaching two throughout the month of October. One in the middle of the day, from ten a.m. to noon, and one in the evenings from seven to nine.

He added his name to slot number fifteen in the evening class, and then he signed Marie up for a kid's art class on Wednesdays that he'd have to ask Natalie to take her to.

As he thought about his large hands trying to make a delicate pie crust, he smiled. Natalie would definitely have her work cut out to make him a baker. He'd learn to make cherry, apple, pumpkin, and pecan pie, only one of which he even liked. He didn't care. It was two hours every week that Natalie couldn't walk away from him, and if she wouldn't go out with him, the cooking class was the next best thing.

He finally heaved himself away from his thoughts and out of bed. Owen went through his day-off morning routine, which ended with him in the backyard, a thermos of coffee at his side. His guitar lay across his lap as Tar Baby sniffed around the yard for the perfect spot to do his business.

Owen picked up the guitar, his fingers so natural on the strings that he didn't have to think about what chords to play or what notes to sing. He'd done both so often, for so long, playing and singing was almost like breathing.

He hadn't played in a few days—since reuniting with Natalie—and she had somehow infused herself into every part of his life. He found himself humming the song he'd written for her while they dated in high school. He'd been planning to sing it at their wedding, and though he'd written dozens of songs since then, this one would never leave his memory.

There were times I thought I'd find you
Right where I left you so long ago
But I drive by and you're not there
Without you, time moves so slow.

I'm down on my luck; I'm not wrong
I'm down on my luck because you're still gone.

His voice rang through the clear, cold morning. As he finished, the notes hung in the air, the chords from his guitar floated toward the heavens. A sense of loss so fierce Owen didn't know how to categorize it sliced through him.

He'd loved deeply before, even if he was only eighteen-years-old at the time. And he hadn't felt that way about anyone since, not even Clarissa, the woman he'd managed to propose to.

With his guitar still slung over his shoulder, he hung his

head and searched for the right thing to do. He had a lot of people counting on him. Marie. His boys. He felt responsible to make sure Marie had her grandparents—both sets—in her life. Responsible to make sure the boys he cared for knew he, well, cared about them.

But he had never told any of them—not even Marie—that he loved them. It was a weakness of his he hadn't been able to overcome since leaving Gold Valley.

He'd only told one person that in his entire life. And now she wouldn't even go out with him.

———

Owen hikes at a steady pace behind Natalie, the sweet sound of her singing voice wafting back to him as they climb toward her favorite spot above the waterfalls. They'd discovered the flat area about the size of a football field at the beginning of the summer, just after the end of their junior year.

She loves the view, the pine trees towering above and below them, the way she can see into the sky forever. Owen loves the way she loves simple things, loves hiking with him, loves...him.

You're going to tell her today, *he promises himself for the tenth time since waking that morning. He's been meaning to tell Natalie that he's in love with her for weeks—since he realized it for certain at the Fourth of July parade at the beginning of the month.*

But he's having a hard time articulating it. In another month, they'll start their senior year, and his plans to go to Nashville are coming together already. He's talked with her about that, about what she'll do after graduation, what their life together will be like.

He just hasn't been able to say those three little words.

They stick in his throat as they near the crest of the path. He slows, trying to buy himself a few more seconds. He's not sure why it makes him so nervous. He's been dating Natalie for almost two years now, and everyone assumes they'll get married come next summer.

Even Owen assumes that, though he and Natalie haven't quite made it that far in their discussions about the future.

He joins her at the top of the hill, his breathing as quick as hers. "Made it," she says through her breathing.

He grins and pulls her into his side. "Never any doubt about that."

"Oh, I was worried." She snakes her hands around his waist and leans into his chest. "You've never brought your guitar before. I thought maybe the added weight would keep you from making it to the top."

He tips his face toward that sky she loves so much and laughs. Hand in hand, they move toward a cropping of rocks in the shade where they can sit, eat the lunches they packed, and waste the afternoon kissing. At least that's what's on Owen's mind. Food and fun.

"Hey, there's water over here."

He pulls himself from his fantasies and focuses on the water, moving right up to the edge of it. "Look at that. Seems too dry for a pool." The rocks seep water as if a natural spring lives beneath, and Owen leans forward to touch his fingers to the cold, damp stone.

THE COWBOY AND THE NANNY

A thrill runs down his spine when Natalie presses in next to him, stepping into the water completely. "It hasn't rained in a month."

Owen glances down as he steps into the cool water too, distracted momentarily by the scrap of fabric Natalie calls shorts and the long legs that extend from them.

Tell her now.

He threads his fingers through hers, his heart thundering through his chest like a herd of wild horses. "Nat," he whispers. "There's something I want to tell you."

She twists into him, her expression open and playful. "What is it?"

He takes her in his arms and presses her into the rocks behind her. "I—" He searches her face, but can't find what he's looking for. He doesn't know what he's looking for. He touches his lips to hers, the familiar fireworks sparking instantly.

She kisses him back, tracing her fingers through his hair and along his shoulders. After a few seconds, she giggles. "This is nice and all," she whispers. "But what did you want to tell me?"

He swallowed, the taste of her chapstick in his mouth now. "I'm—I'm in love with you, Nat." He smiles, the joy of his words infusing his very being. "I love you."

Her eyes widen for a fraction of a second. She gasps as she sucks in a breath. Then her features dissolve into happiness too. "Owen," she says breathlessly, and he wants to hear her say his name like that every day of his life. Now. Always. "I love you too."

He kisses her again, and this time feels different. It feels like the first time all over again. He deepens the kiss, and she gladly goes with him, the grip she maintains on his shoulders as exciting as the moan she emits as he traces his lips down to her throat.

Owen has never known joy like he feels now, and he hopes he'll be able to hold onto it, remember it, cherish it, for a long time to come.

CHAPTER 9

*O*wen played the same song now as he did on that day he'd first told Nat he loved her. They'd spent the afternoon exactly as he'd hoped. Sandwiches, songs, and whispered promises to each other.

When the lyrics became too much and the past too haunting, Owen set aside his guitar and went into the house. He needed to wake Marie for school anyway. After he roused her and she started getting dressed, he went into his bedroom to check his phone.

The light flashed green at the top, and his heart pulsed once with it. He should've taken it outside with him. It didn't happen often, but sometimes his boys or the weekend counselor needed him.

But it was Natalie, and she'd texted the previous night. *I'd love to go out with you. Call me tomorrow and we can schedule something.*

The words burned his eyes. Was she serious? He didn't

see any reason why she wouldn't be. He also didn't see how she'd be up at seven-thirty in the morning when she'd sent this message so late last night.

He flew into gear, first using his cologne before exiting the bedroom to hurry Marie. He packed her lunch and fed her breakfast, his pulse wreaking havoc the whole time. By the time he dropped her off at school, Owen couldn't stop smiling.

He pulled up to Nat's house fifteen minutes later, the clock now reading eight-thirty. He texted her that he'd love to take her to breakfast that morning and could she do that?

She didn't answer, and he went through why that would be. Maybe she didn't have her phone with her. Maybe it was silenced. Maybe she was still in bed.

Feeling restless and impatient, he crossed the lawn and knocked on the front door. Not loudly, but certainly not quietly either. If she were awake, she'd hear it.

She didn't come.

With his heart sinking to his boots, he trudged back to his truck. He breathed deep and employed his patience. He could wait. She wouldn't sleep forever—and he had until three-fifteen before he needed to be back at Marie's school.

After a half an hour of reading the Internet headlines and surfing on social media sites he hadn't touched in months, his patience ran dry. Just as he was about to go bang down the front door, his phone chimed.

She'd texted.

Where are you? After sending the text to Owen, Natalie finger-combed her hair out of her face, trying to contain her smile—and failing. Owen wanted to go to breakfast. She should've known he wouldn't want to wait until Friday night. He never was one to wait when he knew what he wanted. She was just surprised she was what he wanted, and part of her cautioned her to go slow. After all, just a couple of days ago, he'd all but said he wasn't interested in her.

Everything with him seemed so complicated, and yet, she was willing to navigate through the minefield if he was the prize.

Sitting in my truck in front of your house.

Panic poured through her in waves and she whipped her head toward the window, though it was covered by closed blinds.

How long have you been here?

A while.

Her heart warmed and that smile seemed stuck to her face. She hadn't had a man waiting to see her in a very long time, and it felt good. It felt right.

You can come in, she said. *I just got up, and I have to shower. But I can be ready in a half an hour.*

Front door's locked.

She thumbed the call button, and when he answered, she said, "Did you try to break into my house?"

"I'm surprised the front door is locked," he said. "No one locks their doors in Gold Valley."

"Trying to keep the riffraff out," she joked.

"You can be ready in half an hour?"

"Nice change of topic." She stood and went into her bathroom. "And yes, I can be ready in half an hour. I'm in the bathroom, door locked, so it's safe to come in."

"Garage code?"

She hesitated for a moment before saying, "Zero-eight-one-one."

"Zero-eight-one...." The importance of the date dawned on him, obviously, and Natalie waited for him to say something.

"Natalie." He didn't sound upset, or sad. Maybe curious or reproving. It was hard to tell.

She shrugged, though he wasn't there to see her. "Some dreams die hard, Owen. I'm getting in the shower now." She hung up before she could say more, before they could truly talk about why she used the date they'd chosen to get married as her garage code.

A lot of codes, actually, including the parental controls on her television and the PIN number for her debit card. But she wasn't going to tell him that today.

Twenty-five minutes later, thank you very much, she strolled down the hall to find Owen sitting in her living room, the TV on in front of him. She brushed something invisible from the hem of her skirt, which fell to her knee, and adjusted her denim jacket though it already lay in the right place. "Morning," she said.

Owen turned and stood all in one movement, as graceful and fluid as ever. He drank her in from the top of her head to her bare feet and licked his lips. "Mornin'." He tipped his hat to her, a real gentlemanly gesture, and moved closer.

"You look real nice."

"You don't look so bad yourself." He wore jeans and cowboy boots—his usual. He also had a jacket on, zipped most of the way up so she could only see a patch of gray T-shirt underneath. "New hat?"

"Just one I haven't worn in a while."

She grinned, reached up and flicked the brim, and brought her gaze back to his. "It's nice. I like the gray."

He leaned forward like he might kiss her, something she'd seen him do hundreds of times before. She inhaled sharply, and he flinched away from her. While she'd thought about kissing him—a lot actually—the idea of actually doing it made her muscles knot.

"So, are you feeling adventurous?" he asked, putting even more distance between them.

She laughed, the sound filling her house where it got trapped in the corners. "Oh boy. Last time you asked me that, we ended up running from a pair of dogs and vaulting over a fence that had razor wire at the top."

He chuckled. "Totally worth it though."

"Was it?" She shouldered her purse. "I can't quite remember."

"It was," he insisted. "You loved those fresh peas, if memory serves, and we got to the party faster."

"I had to repent about those peas." She giggled. "Pastor Palmer told me to never steal again, and I haven't."

"Well, that's not true," he said as she passed him on her way to the front door.

She swung back to him. "What do you mean?"

A ruddiness entered his cheeks, even through the beard he hadn't shaved since last Friday. "Nothing," he said quickly, gesturing her out the door. "Let's go. I've been up since five and I'm starving."

CHAPTER 10

*N*atalie felt the weight of every eye on her and Owen as they entered the diner. She should've been more prepared for this, but she wasn't. It hadn't even crossed her mind. But now that she sat in a booth across from him, it seemed every able-bodied gossip was having breakfast on that Monday morning.

"So," she said, her voice wavering the slightest bit. "I don't really know what's going on."

Owen's eyes darkened as he lifted his coffee mug to his lips. He sipped, swallowed, smiled. "I don't either. It's kinda nice not to have everything planned out."

"It's terrifying," she admitted.

His phone buzzed, and he flipped it to silent and put it facedown on the table. "It's sort of how I live my life now." He glanced up at the waitress and ordered the steak and eggs. Natalie chose the build-your-own-breakfast and got scrambled eggs, hashbrowns, pancakes, and bacon. Once the waitress left, she leaned her elbows on the table and gazed at Owen.

"I signed up for your pie class," he said.

"You did?"

"Yeah, I thought maybe I'd give it a try this year. I usually just go to my mom's, but…." He shrugged. "This year, I'm taking Marie down to Idaho Falls to see her other grand-parents."

"You are?" The surprises never stopped with Owen. "That's really nice of you."

"I feel a responsibility to make sure she knows them," he said. "I mean, if Henry was still alive, they'd go there for holidays." He spoke evenly, but he swallowed a couple of times after he finished speaking.

"So you thought you'd take them a pumpkin pie, is that it?"

"Actually, anything but pumpkin."

"Why not pumpkin?"

"I really don't like pumpkin pie."

She blinked at him and allowed a giggle to escape. "Well, how very un-American of you. Apple?"

He shook his head, a sexy smirk riding his lips. She suddenly couldn't look anywhere else. "Cherry then."

"Not a fan."

She couldn't figure out why he'd signed up for her class. "That's all we're doing at the class."

"The sign-up sheet said pecan too."

"Oh, that's right. Pecan. I guess that's traditional." She squeezed her lemon in her water as the waitress brought their food. She picked up the bottle of ketchup and slathered her potatoes with it before spreading the ball of butter all over her pancakes.

He was cutting into his steak when she asked, "So if you don't like apple, cherry, or pumpkin pie, what's your favorite kind?"

"Chocolate," he said without hesitation.

She should've known and said as much.

"Some things about me haven't changed," he said. "Most things, actually."

She disagreed, but she didn't say so. The more they talked, the more she learned about him, the more the past version she'd known of him merged with the muscled man before her. They finished, and he paid, and as they walked out of the diner, he captured her hand in his.

"Thanks for coming on short notice," he said. "What are you doing tonight?"

She had no plans, unless cooking a meal for one and then putting on a romantic comedy counted as plans. And they didn't. But she didn't want to tell him that, didn't want him to think she did nothing but putz around the house, eat, and watch chick flicks.

Before she could answer, Owen said, "Oh, no." The level of concern in his voice made her glance at his phone, where he was still looking.

"What?" she asked.

"It's Marie." He met her eyes with panic in his. "Her principal called twice. I need to get over to the school."

"Let's go." She'd never been afraid while in the car with

Owen, but she was now. He pulled up to the curb in the circle drive at the school, barely cutting the ignition before he leapt from the cab. Natalie wasn't sure what to do, but she wasn't going to run to keep up with him. She let him enter the school alone, determined to be a support for him —and Marie—once they got back.

———

Owen cursed himself up one side and down the other. He shouldn't have silenced his phone. He shouldn't have allowed himself to get caught up with Natalie. He had a child to take care of!

"Morning," he said, trying to catch his breath. "Is Miss Teller in? I got two calls from her. Something about Marie Adams?"

"You must be Mister Carr."

"I am."

The secretary flashed him a warm smile as she stood. "She's fine, Mister Carr. Well, she says her stomach hurts, and she's been crying a bit. But she's safe."

Owen's concern spiked. He didn't even know how to take care of a stomachache. "Has she thrown up?"

The secretary nodded and said, "Twice," sympathetically as she moved toward a doorway just around the corner. "I think Miss Teller wanted to meet you, that's why she called." She poked her head into the principal's office. "Miss Teller, Mister Carr is here for Marie." She waved for him to go right in, which he did.

A petite woman about his mother's age stood from behind her desk. "Mister Carr. Nice to meet you." She wore a pleasant smile, along with a navy pencil skirt and a pink blouse.

"I'm so sorry I didn't answer my phone," he apologize. "I was...out."

Miss Teller waved away his worry. "It's fine. I called because just before Marie was sick for the first time, she told me she'd been having trouble with a boy in her class." She perched on the edge of her desk. "I wasn't sure if you were aware of the problem."

"No," he said. "No, I'm not aware. She hasn't said anything at home."

"I was unsure if she was really sick, or if she just wanted to go home because this boy had teased her."

A rage Owen didn't quite understand rushed through his head. "What's happening?"

"I spoke with the boy, and his mother, and apparently, he's been chasing Marie on the playground, tugging on her hair, that kind of thing. He has not hurt her, and he doesn't call her names. I think it's a crush."

Owen nodded, because he wasn't sure what else to do. "Where is she now?"

"Missy's getting her from the nurse's office." Miss Teller straightened. "I just wanted you to know about the boy, Mister Carr, so you feel safe sending Marie to school. I've spoken with him and his mother about how we can't touch someone else without their permission. Though he hasn't hurt Marie, it isn't okay for him to pull on her ponytail."

"Right, okay," Owen said. He wasn't concerned about the other boy. He wanted to see Marie, make sure she was okay. His brain buzzed with what he could do to ease her discomfort, both emotional and physical. He'd probably need to run to the store. But how could he leave Marie alone?

In that moment, he realized that Natalie wasn't standing next to him. Of course she wasn't—she had no legal claim on Marie. *She can help you*, he thought as the secretary came through the door with Marie.

"Marie." Owen dropped to his knees and ran his hands up the girl's arms. She looked pale and shaky. "What's wrong, sweetheart?"

"I don't feel good, Uncle Owen." A single tear trailed down her face and broke his heart.

He stood and scooped her into his arms. "Well, let's go home, baby doll." He glanced at the two women, who both watched him with compassion. "Do I need to sign her out?"

Miss Teller waved. "Just take her home, Mister Carr. Thank you for coming over."

He nodded at them both and held Marie tight against his chest as they exited the building. This parenting gig wasn't for the faint of heart, and the sight of Natalie waiting at the front of his truck brought him more comfort than he knew he needed.

"She's sick," he said when he got closer. "Stomachache." She opened the door for him, and Owen slid Marie into the middle of the bench seat. He straightened and closed the door, leaning close to Natalie so he could take a deep breath of her perfume. She smelled as powdery and fresh as she always had, and Owen's hands found hers.

"Will you come home with me?" he asked. "I have no idea what to do for a stomachache, and I might need to run to the store."

"Well, how can a girl refuse that offer?" She giggled, squeezed his fingers, and stretched up to kiss his cheek before stepping around him and pulling open the passenger-side door again. By the time he got his heavy feet to move, Natalie had Marie's head in her lap. She hummed a song to her as she stroked her hair.

Owen watched them both, and a flash of his future stole through his mind. Could this really be his life? What did he need to do to make it so?

Tell her why you left town, came into his mind, and he felt like crying as he drove carefully back to his house.

CHAPTER 11

Owen did have to go to the store—twice. Once for ginger ale and children's stomach medication. Once for milk and potatoes so Natalie could make shepherd's pie. He should've gotten a bag of frozen peas while he was there, because the one she found way in the back of his freezer tasted like they'd been there since he moved in.

He still ate the food, because Natalie made it and he didn't have anything else. Tar Baby had sensed Marie's distress and had lain by her on the couch since she'd come home. Owen had watched her, taken her temperature every half hour, and kept her favorite cartoons on the television. Natalie had kept him company and then made lunch.

Now, he dozed in the recliner in the living room, everything around him a dull roar. His head ached, but he didn't have the energy to go get something to make it stop.

"I have to go," Natalie whispered.

Owen's eyes jerked open. "You do?"

"Yeah, I teach dance on Monday afternoons, and I don't have any of my clothes or shoes."

He'd picked her up, and though her house was only a five-minute drive, it would be a fifteen-minute walk. "Take my truck," he said. "I'll take you home tonight after she goes to bed." He looked at the snoozing Marie and stood. He gathered Natalie close, close, and whispered, "Thank you for your help today."

She relaxed into him, and Owen was reminded of how easy it had been to be with her. "Thanks for taking me to breakfast." She smiled up at him, but didn't move to kiss him again. She stepped away from him, and he let her go, his arms empty and his world cold without her.

After she left with his keys in her hand, he collapsed back into the recliner. He felt as though he was walking on thin ice, on a lake that had no bottom. One wrong step, and he'd fall in. While part of that excited him, tempted him to take one more step, the rational side of him screamed to get off the ice. Get off the ice quickly.

But he didn't want to. He wanted to spend time with Natalie, heal what he'd done to her, discover what could potentially make him happy.

It just couldn't happen at the expense of Marie.

"Just don't turn off your phone again," he mumbled as he leaned back and closed his eyes. He slept, his dreams filled with wide, blue skies and a woman with hazel-gold eyes.

———

Natalie's toes paid the price of her frustration. She'd told Owen she'd bring his truck back after her dance classes, but she hadn't. When she'd finished teaching, she'd stayed at the studio, at the barre, with her pointe shoes on. She hadn't danced at all that day, and whipping up a shepherd's pie hadn't adequately drained the emotion from the muscles in her neck.

She rolled her head from side to side, still feeling some tension along her shoulders. She wasn't surprised. Starting a new relationship with any man would have her on-edge. The fact that he was Owen actually made things more stressful. She couldn't exactly pinpoint why, but she felt it.

Pastor Palmer had spoken on embracing the gospel on Sunday. He'd mentioned that sometimes people take for granted what they have. She'd been thinking a lot about what he'd said, and not just in temporal terms. She was grateful for every dollar she had, and she always had been. She didn't have many skills that would make her much money, and she'd relied on credit cards when things needed to stretch.

Problem was, those credit cards had to be paid back. During and after the sermon, she'd sent thanks to God for the job with Owen. Because of it, she could finally get out from under the pile of debt she'd created for herself.

He'd challenged them not to take their faith for granted, and she'd been thinking about it ever since. Did she just expect her faith to be there when she needed it? Was faith something she simply possessed but didn't have to foster, develop, or grow?

Pastor Palmer had suggested that faith needed caring for, and that he'd seen faithful members neglect the care and feeding of their faith. So Natalie sat cross-legged, alone in the studio, and pulled up the scriptures on her phone. She read for a few minutes. Read until the tension and aches and worries of the day fled.

She then sent a text to Owen: *I'll bring your truck back in the morning when I come to watch Marie. Do you think she'll go to school tomorrow?*

And: *I liked spending the day with you.* Warmth filled her heart at the memory of the day. Owen had been so stressed about Marie, and Natalie had been able to help him. A small miracle she thanked the Lord for as she typed out another text.

What do you want for dinner tomorrow night?

His response was classic Owen, mashing all his answers into a single message.

That's fine about the truck. Yes, she'll go. She's doing better now. I liked seeing you today too. Whatever you want.

She smiled, her thumbs flying over the keyboard when another message came in.

I didn't just like seeing you today. I really liked talking with you and holding your hand. Stay for dinner tomorrow?

She deleted what she'd typed and simply said *Sure.*

She was less sure when his next text read, *I need to tell you about why I left the day after graduation, okay?*

In fact, a cold pit opened in her chest, and it was filled with darkness and sadness. She'd spent that entire first summer without him bathed in shadows and doubt, shame and disbelief. She'd cried a lot. Hiked to their spot on the mountain. Sent him emails and texts he answered in vague, one-word sentences.

Life had marched forward, but she'd never really moved on. She'd dated other men, but she'd never gotten over Owen.

Back then, she'd so desperately wanted him to tell he why he'd left without her, but now, she wasn't so sure she needed to know.

She pulled into his driveway at five-twenty-five and left the truck running. The heater wasn't blowing warm air yet, and she pulled her jacket closed at the throat. An autumn breeze blew, signaling the beginning of winter, and she shuddered involuntarily. She sure hated the snow and cold for someone who chose to live in it for six months out of the year.

She didn't knock, and his front door wasn't locked when she entered. She shivered when she shut the wind out, and he poked his head out from behind the wall in the kitchen. "Hey, there." His face split into a smile. "Cold this mornin', right?"

"Winter's coming," she confirmed. "Is that coffee?"

"Cream in the fridge."

"You don't drink cream in your coffee."

"I sure don't." He trailed his fingers down her arm, sending a different kind of shiver through her system.

"Then why do you have it in your fridge?" She poured herself a cup of coffee, relishing the warmth from the steam as it drifted upward.

He pulled her close, and said, "For you." His lips brushed her hairline, making all her thoughts evaporate. "And Marie likes it on her cereal." He released her with a chuckle. He swiped his jacket from the hook by the backdoor. "Okay, so you're dancing until seven tonight?"

She groaned. "Oh, yeah. I was planning to make chicken Alfredo for dinner. I can make it tomorrow. How do you feel about Chinese takeout?"

He wrinkled his nose, triggering her memories. "Oh, that's right. You dislike food you can't eat with a fork."

"It's awkward." He zipped his jacket all the way to his throat, covering his black and white striped shirt.

"You know you can just use the silverware you want. Chopsticks aren't required."

"So you've told me a thousand times."

"And yet you won't even try the tangy chicken from Pan's."

"I'll pick something up on the way home," he said. "Something you like."

"Better not be burgers," she called after him as he headed for the front door. "I mean, you can't eat those with a fork."

"You're so funny," he said, but his voice did broadcast a playful tone. "See you tonight."

"Wait," she said, and he turned back. "Will you stop by the studio and get Marie too? Or will she be staying with me the whole time? It doesn't matter either way, I'll just get her prepared with her homework, her tablet, all of that, depending on how long she'll be there with me."

"I'll grab her too." He smiled, tipped that new gray

cowboy hat, and stepped into the morning darkness. In Owen's absence, Tar Baby came padding into the kitchen. He sniffed around Natalie's feet before licking her ankle. She yelped and pushed the dog back.

She left her coffee untouched on the counter and settled into Owen's couch for another couple of hours of sleep.

CHAPTER 12

"And one, and two, and three." Natalie moved along the front of the room. "Lift those arms, Jade. And kick, kick, kick." The seven-year-old class was her favorite, because they'd been in dance classes for a few years and could keep up with the choreography she used.

It was her second class of the night, and Marie sat in the corner completely entranced with these girls. The first class had been four-year-olds, and Marie had spent most of that class on her tablet. But these girls were more her age, and Natalie determined to ask Owen about enrolling Marie in the class.

She moved over to the stereo system and paused the music. "Combo two, girls." She tapped on her music player to the next song. "Get high on those toes now. Be sure to hold the arms at the right position." She lifted hers. "Right to the side. Left over the head." She tapped the player. "And go."

The music began and the girls danced with Natalie calling out corrections and praise. "Beautiful, Charlotte," she said as the music ended. She paused it to give more instructions, but Owen stuck his head into the room. Every eye turned in his direction. After all, not many cowboys stopped by the studio.

"Evenin' girls," he drawled. "Nat, is Marie—?" He stopped as his niece stood and hurried toward him. She giggled as he swooped her into a hug. "See you at home, okay, Nat?"

She nodded, Stephanie hovering on the other side of the glass. She turned away from him as he turned to leave, her voice only a tiny bit shaky as she said, "Combo two again, ladies. Work those calf muscles."

When she finished teaching, she went into the office to turn in her time card for the week. Stephanie was signing hers and glanced up. "Holy smokes, Natalie. You didn't say Owen was dreamy *and* a devoted father."

Natalie sighed, not wanting to have this conversation at the studio. "It was implied."

"Makes him a bit sexier, don't you think?"

Natalie signed her card and set it on the manager's desk. She bumped Stephanie with her shoulder. "I think if he gets any sexier, he'll have to be locked up." She grinned. "Now, I have to go eat dinner with him, so I'll talk to you later."

Stephanie latched onto her arm, her orange-painted nails practically digging into her skin. "You're eating dinner with him?"

"And we went to breakfast yesterday morning."

"So you're dating him." It wasn't a question, and Stephanie's smile was nothing but genuine.

"I suppose so," Natalie said. "We haven't defined it." She shrugged like it was no big deal, but the hand-holding, the hugging, the texting, the sweet kisses they'd shared were all a big deal to Nat.

With a jolt of fear, she realized that if things didn't work out with Owen this time, she'd be devastated. Sure, she'd been heartbroken last time, discouraged, depressed. But she knew one thing for certain—if she and Owen didn't end up married this time, she'd never recover.

So she smiled timidly at Stephanie and drove ten under the speed limit on her way to Owen's. Her mind churned, and her heart warned her to put proper defenses in place so she didn't end up losing everything. At the same time, the possibility existed that she'd get what she'd dreamed of twelve years ago. A family and a life with Owen.

She mounted the steps and knocked at the same time she entered his house. Marie sat on the couch and she jumped up as Natalie entered. "Nat, hi!" She flung her arms around Natalie's waist. "That dance class was really interesting to watch. Uncle Owen says I can sign up if I want to, and I was wondering if I sign up, will you be my teacher?"

Natalie smoothed her hand over the girl's blonde hair. "Yes, sweetheart. You'd be in the six o'clock class." She didn't say that was the beginner's class, though it was. Girls from ages five to eight were in that class, as it was their first time taking ballet.

"Uncle Owen!" Marie tore into the kitchen. "Nat says I'd be in the six o'clock class."

Natalie heard Owen's low voice respond, but she couldn't understand the words. He appeared a moment later, Marie at his side. "Dinner in here." He grinned at her, a secret riding in his eyes.

She stepped in his direction, tucking her hands into her sweatshirt pockets. She wore a pair of joggers over the black leggings she wore to teach and a tank top with flimsy straps under the sweatshirt. She shouldn't be so worried about Owen seeing her in such tight and scant clothing—he already had.

She stepped into the kitchen to see the kitchen counter covered with white Chinese containers. She gaped at the sheer number of them and then switched her gaze to Owen.

"That one there is the tangy chicken." He pointed to one of the open containers. "You were right. It's really good."

"You ate it?"

"I can try new things." He glanced at Marie, who stood watching their exchange. "Hey, sweetheart, it's time to get in the tub."

"You said I could have another fortune cookie when Nat got here."

He chuckled as he reached for a cookie. "I sure did. Now go on. *You* said you'd take a bath and finish your homework when Nat got here."

Something zinged through her when she realized that the two of them had included her in their lives. She picked up a plate and started scooping herself some of the tangy chicken she liked. By the time she'd filled her plate, the water was running in the bathroom and Owen had seated himself at the kitchen table.

She sat across from him, a slip of nervous energy eliminating her appetite because of the serious glint in his eye. "Good day?" she asked.

"Good enough. You?"

She forked in a mouthful of rice and chicken and nodded. "I prepped my first pie class. I hope you're ready to get your hands on some dough."

A twinkle entered his eye, but it only stayed for half a heartbeat. "Natalie," he said. "I need to tell you why I left Montana early."

Her throat closed though she'd only taken two bites. She pushed her food away. "If you have to."

"I thought you wanted to know."

"I do—I did. I don't know."

"You don't know?"

"You're not that great at explaining things," she said, following her words with, "I mean, you're great with horses and bossing around boys—"

"I do *not* boss anyone around."

She placed her hand on his, hoping to placate him. "I didn't mean it like that."

"So I'm not the only one who struggles with saying what they mean."

She gave him a smirk and folded her arms. "What I meant is you're really good at some things. Explaining to me what you want and why you do things isn't necessarily one of them."

He swallowed and raked one hand through his hair. As he settled his cowboy hat back into place, he said, "Well, I want to try. No, I *need* to try."

"Go on, then."

He took a big breath, so big she thought sure his lungs would burst. He released it in a slow hiss. "All right. The simple, short answer is that I panicked."

She blinked, unsure of what he wanted her to say in response to that.

"I was afraid that if I waited to leave Gold Valley, that I never would. That I'd never get to Nashville. And I panicked. I packed in the middle of the night, and I left as soon as it got light. I drove there in one day, only stopping for gas, for fear that if I even stopped to spend the night in a hotel, that I wouldn't make it to Nashville." He paused as Tar Baby came up and pushed his nose against Owen's leg.

"I'm okay, boy," he said, scrubbing the dog's head.

"There's no way you could drive that distance in one day," she said. "We planned everything, Owen, right down to where we'd stay and how many hours you'd drive before I took over. It was four days of driving."

"I drove all day, and all night. I got to Nashville about noon the day after I left. I didn't stop. The panic was that real."

She'd felt panic like that once too—when she'd discovered he'd left without her. She clamped her lips around that confession and let him continue.

"I can see now that I was irrational, but I couldn't then. I truly believed that if I didn't go right then and there, I wouldn't go at all. And that wasn't an option for me."

"I texted you and called you and emailed you." She didn't realize how much hurt still writhed within her, but it echoed in her voice.

"I know." He sighed and took off his cowboy hat. He set it on the table between them, and when he looked at her again, he seemed more vulnerable. More human. He had a full head of beautiful brown hair that made Natalie's fingers itch to touch it. He pushed it back off his forehead and closed his eyes.

"I was embarrassed," he confessed. "I didn't know what to tell you, so I didn't say much of anything."

"I would've come."

"Your father would've killed me. Heck, my father almost killed me."

She looked away as tears pricked her eyes. She'd never told him that she *had* tried to follow him, that her father had stopped her, that he had been very, very angry with her. She told him now, and he listened raptly, his hand curling around hers when she ended with, "So that's why I couldn't come. My father kept the keys locked up, and he took my debit card, and basically all I had was my phone." She took a shuddering breath. "He said there would be other boys, but there weren't." Employing every ounce of bravery she possessed, she added, "Owen, there's never been anyone but you."

His chair scraped against the floor as he got up and knelt

in front of her. His warm, rough hands cupped her face and tucked the wayward strands of her hair behind her ear. "For me either, Nat."

She nodded, which caused a tear to splash onto her cheek. He wiped it with his thumb, the action tender and kind. He smiled at her with sadness in the gesture. "I'm so sorry, sweetheart."

She sat ramrod straight, not daring to relax into him, to give away an inch of her composure now that she'd already cried. "Did you ever want to come back?"

"At first, no," he admitted. "But not because I didn't want to see you. Only because I hadn't gotten my record deal yet. I'm a selfish man, Natalie. I know that. I'm sorry."

She wanted to tell him that he wasn't selfish, that he was driven, that he'd done what he'd always dreamed of doing. She, on the other hand, had only left town after she was certain Owen wasn't coming back, couldn't pay her bills, and hadn't auditioned for the Gold Valley ballet company the way she'd dreamed of doing.

"I don't think you're selfish," she finally said, boxing up her own failures and shoving them onto a shelf to deal with later. "Someone who's selfish wouldn't have taken in an eight-year-old child. I heard you had to give up your cabin at Silver Creek. You've had to rearrange a lot in your life to be her dad."

He retook his seat, his expression unreadable. "I haven't given up as much as you think I have."

"Doesn't matter. You're doing what you have to do. For her." She studied the wood grain in the table.

He cleared his throat. "Anyway, I thought about coming back for you a hundred times. And when I signed my deal, you were the only one I wanted to share it with. Remember I emailed you?"

"I remember." Her whisper tickled her tongue, and she swallowed to get her voice to work properly.

"And after that, I was busy. Busy writing songs. Busy recording. Busy working on the art of making music. It was twenty-four-seven work."

"But you loved it."

"I did love it."

She looked at him and found adoration on his face. Adoration and agony. She wanted to comfort him, but she felt like they were both patients in the hospital. Both bleeding. Both in need of medical attention, and she didn't have anything to give him. If anything, she needed his reassurances to keep breathing.

"I know you said things got messed up with your manager," she said. "But why didn't you just get another one and make another record? Why come home when you had the whole world in the palm of your hand?"

———

The ache in Owen's gut intensified. He didn't want to get into all the particulars of his relationship with Clarissa. She'd been awful at her job, lost him a lot of money, and skipped town with his heart.

But not his whole heart, and he knew it. Had always

LIZ ISAACSON

known it. So yes, he'd been broken because of her, but not because she wasn't his girlfriend anymore.

"I could've done that," he said. "But honestly, I'd had enough. I had a bestselling record. A number one country music single. I didn't have friends in Nashville, not real ones. Not people I could count on if my truck broke down or I suddenly had a daughter to take care of."

He appreciated the steadiness of Natalie's gaze, though she seemed rigid and wooden. Those eyes sucked at him, begged him to be real and truthful.

"So I came home. I had plenty of money, and I found I didn't care. Happiness doesn't come from how much you have in your bank account."

She half-coughed, half-choked and he saw something run through her eyes he didn't understand.

"I was worried about how my parents would receive me. But they were forgiving and kind. Tasha too." His voice almost broke on his sister's name, but he managed to steady it. "She and Henry had Marie, and she was a year old, and I'd never met her. I have way more here than I ever had in Nashville."

"And why didn't you ever get in touch with me after you came back?"

"I had no hope that you'd even speak to me. I couldn't stomach the rejection, so it was easier to stay away. I knew I'd messed up, and badly, and I didn't want to face you." He smiled at her. "But here you are anyway, and I'm not sorry about that. I'm only sorry it took seven more years to get you here."

All at once, Owen understood something he'd been puzzling through for six months. He didn't understand why God had taken Tasha and Henry at the same time. Didn't understand why Marie had to grow up with only memories and stories of them. He'd asked God why she had to suffer her whole life, and he'd come up blank every time.

But now, he had at least one reason. Could God have allowed one tragedy to happen in order to bring Natalie back into his life? He believed that the Lord put people in his life who needed to be there, exactly when they needed to be there. And he certainly needed Natalie's help with Marie.

He wouldn't lie and say his sister's death hadn't affected his faith. It had. He felt removed from the Lord, though he still prayed, still went to church, still believed. He just felt... distant. Like a layer of waxed paper existed between him and God.

Owen glanced up as he heard Marie's footsteps coming down the hall. She dragged her backpack with her, and he reached for it to check her homework.

"I'll comb out your hair, sweetheart," Natalie said, her voice a tick on the thick side.

Owen checked the homework while Natalie brushed Marie's hair, and everything that had been askew in his life righted itself. He loved Marie, and he'd take care of her for the rest of his life. But he also wanted a child of his own. A daughter with hazel-gold eyes like Natalie's.

His thoughts both surprised and embarrassed him, so he kept his gaze on the math paper though the numbers blurred together. "This looks great." He shoved the paper into her backpack and gestured for her to come to him. She did, and he pulled her into a tight hug. "Great job, baby doll." He held onto her shoulders as he moved her away from him a little so he could look directly into her eyes. "I love you, Marie."

He wasn't sure if she'd noticed that he'd never told her he loved her. Now, her face burst into a smile and she hugged him again. "Love you too, Uncle Owen."

He cleared his throat. "Should we play a game tonight? Or do you want to watch another movie?"

"Can we play Pictionary?" She glanced at Natalie and back to Owen, who groaned.

"I'm no good at Pictionary," he said. "You always beat me."

Marie giggled as she skipped down the hall to her room. "I'll get the pens." She disappeared into her room and then popped her head back out. "I get Nat on my team."

Owen exhaled as he stood and put his cowboy hat back on. "Dang," he said quietly. "I was hoping Nat would be on my team." She stood too, and he eased his hands around her waist. "Thank you for listening to me tonight."

She held onto his arms and gazed up at him. "Thanks for explaining."

He wanted to lean down and kiss her. It felt like the time to do it, but Marie returned, and Owen put the required distance between him and Natalie, hoping another time would present itself before she left.

An hour later, Marie had won Pictionary again. "All right, time for bed." He capped the purple gel pen he'd been using—unsuccessfully—to draw a chicken nugget. Marie and Natalie were still giggling over his pathetic rendition of the popular snack food, and his eyes had started feeling like someone had rubbed sand in them twenty minutes ago.

"Go on and brush your teeth," he said. "I'll come tuck you in in a minute."

Natalie put the Chinese food containers in the fridge and wiped down the counter. "I should go. Five o'clock comes so early."

"Tell me about it." He flashed her a smile and held up one finger. "Give me a second to tuck her in? I have one more thing to tell you."

She leaned against the counter and waved for him to go on down the hall. He hurried to get Marie into bed and returned to the kitchen, where Tar Baby sat at the backdoor, his eyes set on pleading.

Owen opened the door to let the dog out, and he stepped into the cool night air too. "It's nice tonight," he said over his shoulder. "Come look at the stars."

Natalie exhaled in a way that said, *Really Owen? The stars?* but she joined him. "So what else did you need to tell me?"

His throat went dry, much the same way it did the first time he'd told her he loved her. He wasn't going to say *that* tonight—didn't dare and didn't know if it was all the way true—but the floodgate between them had been busted wide open when he'd told her she was the only one for him.

"I just wanted to say goodnight." He reached for her, pulled her close, held her tight. "I wanted to kiss you goodnight." He let his words hang in the chilly air the way his breath did, waiting for her permission.

"Well you better hurry up and do it then," she said. "We've got to get up early in the morning."

He chuckled as he lowered his lips to hers, all his senses on overdrive. This kiss, though not even close to their first, felt new, and wonderful, and healing. Her sensual touch made him feel whole, something he hadn't experienced in years.

He kneaded her closer, kissed her deeper, fell a little faster.

She pulled back, and he felt like his skin was steaming in the near-winter night. "Wow, Owen." She spoke with undeniable desire in her voice, and he wanted to drive her to that every time he kissed her.

"Yeah." He ran his hands up her back as he traced his lips down her jaw to the hollow of her throat. "Can you believe this is where we are now?"

"You might have to convince me again." Her lips were curved upward when he matched his against them again.

"I can do that," he murmured against her mouth before claiming it for a second kiss.

CHAPTER 13

*W*hat used to be a challenge for Owen—making sure Marie was well-cared for after school and into the evening—quickly became his favorite time. If Natalie wasn't in his house, whipping up something delicious, he got to see her in her spandex clothes teaching ballet.

And he kissed her every chance he got. That desire hadn't changed either, and she seemed to enjoy kissing him every evening before she stumbled out his front door and every morning before he left for work.

His first pie class had been a complete disaster; he hadn't even been able to finish the dough before the end of the class. Thankfully, the class that evening would use the same dough, and Natalie had been practicing with him at home. He just didn't quite know how to make his big hands deal with small things like teaspoons and capfuls.

He left work late, because he'd gotten a new crop of boys

and it always took a couple of weeks to break them in. First, they were away from everything they knew, and that was rough. He'd been called over in the middle of the night three times in the past three weeks.

Second, they had to learn all the rules of Silver Creek, which was challenging enough. No girls, no weapons or drugs, no outside communication. Oh, and talk to someone you don't know about your deepest fears and feelings, never be alone—ever—and eat only three times a day. No snacks. No exceptions.

Third, they had to learn Owen's rules and personality. Some balked at calling him Mister Carr, and others had never even seen a horse in real life. Yes, the first few weeks of a new group of boys could be brutal on everyone involved.

Owen was almost out of that phase now, thankfully, and he only had one boy who hadn't quite gotten all the way onboard. He did his best to put away his work problems before he got home. That was something he'd learned from his father, who worked long hours in a thankless job and Owen had never known it.

He arrived early at the church, a squirrel of excitement racing down his spine when he saw Natalie's black sedan in the parking lot. He went inside and down the hall toward the kitchen, the smell of butter and sugar already loitering in the air.

He found Natalie there, bent over a recipe, her streaked hair falling over her shoulder. "Hey, gorgeous." He slid his arm around her waist and gave her a squeeze.

She grinned at him, but her attention obviously lingered on the recipe. "Hey, you ready for tonight?"

"Not even close." He chuckled. "But I think I might be able to get something resembling a pie this week."

"Anything would be better than last week." She nudged him with her shoulder and gave him a smile.

"Hey." He returned the playful nudge, taking the opportunity to pull her close. He kissed her, taking his time to really explore, to enjoy himself.

"Stop it," she said breathlessly, with no weight behind the words. "People will be here any minute. Behave yourself."

"You kissed me back," he whispered, but he stepped away, the heat in the kitchen already through the roof. "Did you talk to your mom this week?"

"Yeah, she called back this morning right as I dropped Marie off at school. My sister Julie is having Thanksgiving at her place. My parents will be there."

"You gonna go?" He was going to Idaho Falls with Marie to spend some time with Henry's parents.

"I think so. You won't be here, so why not?"

He hadn't invited her to come to Idaho with him. It was still too soon in their relationship, and he barely knew Henry's parents himself. He couldn't take along his girlfriend of a few weeks, and he hadn't had to explain why. Thankfully, Natalie seemed to understand.

"You should go," he said. "Where are they? Boulder?"

"Wrong state." She gave up studying the recipe. "Peach Valley, Wyoming."

"Ah, yes. Wyoming. Why'd your parents move there again?"

"Dad opened a new fried chicken franchise there. He still owns the one here, too, but they were looking for a change, and Julie lived there, so."

"I could go for some fried chicken after this."

Her eyebrows lifted and a fire entered her eyes. Owen backtracked, and fast. "I mean, not that the *delicious* stir fry you made wasn't enough." He just wasn't into vegetables as a main course. He'd never say that out loud to her, though. *Nev*er.

"Get to your station," she said, her tone drier than a desert. He fell back two steps when two women entered the kitchen, chattering away about their teenagers. They spied Owen, and their grins widened.

"How's Marie?" one of them, a woman his mother's age named Penny Partridge, asked.

"She's doin' just fine, ma'am." Owen knew his manners and when to use them.

"How's your momma?" the other asked.

"Right as rain, Miss Gurr. She's watchin' Marie tonight."

"Didn't you hire a nanny?" Penny asked.

"I sure did." Owen cast a glance up to Natalie, but she didn't seem to be paying attention to the conversation.

"Who is it?" Penny sure could be relentless, something Owen should've known from high school. Her son had mentioned it more than once.

"Natalie." Owen nodded toward the front of the kitchen right as Nat looked up.

140

The two women looked back and forth between Natalie, who looked perplexed, and Owen, who couldn't stop grinning.

———

Natalie took extra time to make sure she looked absolutely perfect on Sunday morning. She and Owen had been dating behind closed doors for just over a month. He brought food home on Mondays and Tuesdays, and she cooked the other nights. She rarely left his house earlier than nine-thirty, and even that was way too late.

With her new job, she'd been able to get current on her car payments, give herself a little bit of breathing room. She loved taking care of Marie, loved the little girl to pieces. And she felt herself falling for Owen with every evening they spent together.

She curled another lock of her hair and added a string of pearls around her neck. After the third pie class—where Owen had managed to complete his first edible pie—he'd asked her to sit with him at church.

It was a milestone in their relationship, because she normally sat with her friends. Which meant explanations had to be made. And he normally sat with Marie and his parents. More explanations.

And everyone in town would see them together, and start talking, and suspicions would be raised. Not only that, but he'd asked her to join him and Marie for dinner at his parents' house following church.

She'd said yes, of course. No hesitation. But, oh the fear. She wondered when she wouldn't be so worried about what his mom would think of her, what the ladies in the sewing club were saying about her, when she should tell her own parents about her rekindled relationship with the man they believed had broken her heart.

That was a conversation she wasn't looking forward to, that was for sure. They had liked Owen in high school, and her mom had confessed that she knew Natalie would be marrying him very soon after graduation. But when he'd left like that, he'd lost a lot of credibility in her mother's eyes. And her father had written him off completely.

She hadn't told him any of that, and she hoped that maybe he'd go to Wyoming with her at Christmastime. She'd started praying for that prospect—and for the right way to ease him into the Thanksgiving conversation at the dinner table.

Natalie held her head high as she walked into the chapel, but her fingers clutched her purse a bit too tight to be casual. Hopefully no one would notice.

"Nat." Marie stood halfway toward the front of the chapel, waving for all she was worth. "Come sit by us."

Natalie smiled genuinely at the girl and reached for her hand when she got close enough. "Hey, sweetheart." She glanced down the row, where she found Owen's mother and father—but not Owen. She cast her eyes around, looking for him.

"Pastor Palmer grabbed him," Owen's mother said, a

warm smile on her face. She stood and gave Natalie a hug. "How are you, dear?"

"Just fine, ma'am. How are you?" She looked tired as she stepped back and sat down, and a blip of worry stole through Nat.

"Oh, you know. Taking one day at a time."

"I can imagine." Natalie gave her a compassionate smile and sat down beside her. "I'm so sorry about Tasha and Henry." She patted the older woman's hand, who curled her fingers around Natalie's and squeezed.

"Thank you." She released Natalie but leaned in closer to her ear. "So Owen seems happier these past few weeks."

"Does he?"

"So much happier." His mom straightened and looked at her husband. "Bill, you remember Natalie Lower, don't you?"

"Sure do." He shook her hand and smiled, and Natalie remembered how much she'd liked Owen's parents. He'd said they'd been forgiving and kind when he'd come crawling home, and she could see such charity in them. They were good people, who'd raised a good son.

Owen slid into the row only moments before the service started. "Sorry," he whispered as he snaked his hand along the back of the pew behind Marie, who sat between them. He panted and took a deep drag of air to steady his breathing. "I'll tell you about it later."

She smiled and shifted a little closer to Marie, thus a little closer to Owen. His fingers brushed her shoulder, and heat flamed in her face. Within moments, he'd scooped the girl onto his lap and slid all the way over next to Natalie. He balanced Marie on his left side and lifted his right arm over Natalie's shoulders.

A sense of safety and protection enveloped her, and she managed to ignore the weight of his mother's eyes and instead focused on what the pastor had to say.

He spoke of ways to kindle or rekindle a passion for something or someone. He referenced his sermon from several weeks ago, the one that had prompted Natalie to re-examine her own faith. As she listened to him speak about finding the good things in life and pursuing those, her thoughts turned to ballet.

The sharp taste of regret filled her mouth no matter how much she tried to swallow it away. She was too old now to join the professional ballet company in town, and she suffered through the rest of the sermon though Owen's arm around her was warm and wonderful.

"Marie wants to see if there are any other classes she can take," Owen said once the closing hymn finished. "She loved that art one you brought her to."

"Suzy is a great teacher." Natalie glanced at Marie. "Should we go see what else they have?"

Marie slipped one hand into Nat's and one into Owen's and tugged them toward the aisle. "Yes, let's go."

"All right, turbo," Owen said. He chuckled as he stood and moved into the aisle ahead of Marie. Natalie followed them both, feeling very much like she was part of this family, something she hadn't enjoyed since her parents had moved to Wyoming to start their second franchise.

She hadn't realized how lonely she'd been. Or maybe she had and just didn't know what to do about it.

She lingered at the mouth of the hall where the activity tables stood, relinquishing her grip on Marie's hand so they could go look at the options.

"So I take it you won't be coming to dinner tonight." Stephanie stopped next to her. "I saw you two all cuddling up to each other." She grinned and cast her eyes down the hall to where Owen was bent over the table with Marie.

"I texted you," Natalie said as Owen's parents exited the chapel. "I'm going to Owen's mother's for dinner." She grinned at the woman, who came toward her. "Stephanie, this is Paula Carr and her husband Bill."

"Nice to meet you." Stephanie shook their hands and slipped away. Owen still hadn't returned, and Natalie wondered if making a choice was really that hard.

"Owen said I didn't need to bring anything for dinner," she said. "Is that really true?"

Paula smiled, but the action didn't quite reach her eyes. "Bill?" She glanced back at Natalie. "He does all the cooking."

"Because I'm pretty good in the kitchen," Natalie said. "I teach classes here and everything." She pointed down the hall. "I just finished a pie class, and I'm starting a holiday side dish class this next week."

Owen's father seemed lost inside his own thoughts, and it took him several seconds to focus on her. "Do you bake?"

"Sure." Concern and compassion combined inside her. Owen's parents were really suffering, and she could only assume the cause was the death of their daughter only seven short months ago. "Cookies? Cake? You name it."

He patted her shoulder as he passed, his gaze already out the large windows that flanked the church doors. "Whatever you want, Nat. We eat at four o'clock."

She watched them go, shake Pastor Palmer's hand and begin speaking with him. He watched them with the same apprehension she felt pulling through her, and he didn't release his hold on Paula's hand until she nodded. Natalie thought she saw his mom reach up and wipe her eyes too, but Owen appeared at her side and distracted her.

"All ready."

"What did you pick?" she asked Marie as they stepped toward the exit.

"Your class," she said with excitement. "Uncle Owen said it's on Saturday mornings and I can come." She skipped ahead of them and hugged Pastor Palmer before disappearing outside.

"She was really excited about it, especially the pronto pups." Owen slid his hand around her back and rested his hand on her hip, claiming her in front of everyone. He didn't seem to notice how everyone looked at them, how Pastor Palmer's eyes lingered on the point of contact between them before lifting to Natalie's.

"It's just a corn dog," Natalie said. "You told her that, right?"

"I didn't know that," Owen said. "So, no, I didn't tell her that. Great sermon, Pastor." He shook the man's hand and said he was going to figure out what he was passionate about doing, and do it.

"What about you?" Pastor Palmer gazed at Natalie with his wise eyes, and she realized how much she would miss him once he retired in a couple of months.

"I'm not sure," she answered truthfully. "I missed out on something in my life, but I'm not sure I can still do it." She leaned forward and grinned when the pastor did too. "I'm too old, you know?"

He threw his head back and laughed. "Oh, Miss Natalie, I understand old." He clasped her hand in both of his. "Maybe you'll find something new to pursue." His eyes flicked to Owen.

"I'm sure I will." Natalie moved past him and took Owen's hand as they entered the chilly October air. It had snowed several times already, but the sun had managed to melt it after a few days. Now dark clouds roiled in the sky, and she wondered if this would be a week of cold rain or the first real snowfall of the year. She hoped for the former, her bones already dreading the wind chill that blew down from Canada.

"What were you talkin' about back there?" Owen asked once they'd cleared earshot of the pastor.

"Ballet."

"You're not too old for that."

She laughed, the sound not quite as happy as she'd like it to be. "I totally am, Owen. You realize I should've auditioned in my senior year for the company, right? Most ballerinas are retired by age thirty."

He paused and pulled her close. "I didn't know that, Nat. Sorry." He pressed a kiss to her temple. "At least you're a brilliant chef."

She shoved him playfully in the chest. "Stop it."

"I was being serious." He quirked a smile in her direction and glanced around. "Now, where did Marie get to?"

"She's sitting on your tailgate." Natalie pointed, an idea popping into her head. "Your dad asked me to bring a dessert to dinner. Can I take Marie home with me and we can bake together?"

"I don't see why not. Am I not invited?"

"Nope, not invited." She moved ahead of him and told Marie about their afternoon of baking. "Uncle Owen is going to go home and take a nap or something." She gave him a flirty smile. "What do your grandma and grandpa like?"

"Chocolate," Marie and Owen said at the same time.

"I should've known." She loaded Marie into her car, grinning first at Owen, and then Marie, the two people she was beginning to think she couldn't live without.

CHAPTER 14

"So measure that salt into this bowl." Natalie set the mixing bowl in front of Marie. "One teaspoon. And then one of the baking soda."

She was making her chocolate-chocolate chip cookies, and though she had the recipe memorized, she consulted it to make sure she'd told Marie right. The girl did as she was instructed, and Natalie told her about the dry and wet ingredients. "So the oven is hot, and we're ready to mix. You want to cream the butter and sugar?"

"Yep." She got off the stool Natalie had set up for her and moved it to the corner of the kitchen, where Natalie's stand mixer waited.

"Put it on three or four," Nat said. "I measured in the butter and sugars already."

"Nat," Marie said, her hand poised on the mixer's *on* switch.

"Yeah, sweetie?"

"Are you and Uncle Owen going to get married?"

Natalie blinked, blinked. "I—I don't know."

She frowned, clearly puzzling through something. She switched on the mixer, and her troubles seemed to dash away with the speed of the blade attachment. She didn't ask any more questions that weren't related to cooking, but Natalie couldn't seem to move past the first one.

Would Owen ask her to marry him this time? She couldn't imagine a scenario where she'd refuse him if he did, and a pin of fear pushed into her heart, expanding until she felt like she'd swallowed a sword.

By the time Owen arrived to pick them up for dinner, she'd managed to clear her discomfort, but she still wielded the cookies like shields, like they alone would ward off any unwanted questions about her future with Owen.

———

"Are you sure you're okay?" Owen worried about Natalie. "I know my parents can be a bit much." He'd actually thought dinner had gone well. His mother didn't ask anything embarrassing or that he couldn't answer. Natalie had been charming, and beautiful, and accepting. But something was off. He'd felt it as soon as he'd picked her and Marie up before heading to his parents' for dinner.

"Fine." She twisted toward him, and his hand fell from her shoulder to her upper arm. "Are your parents okay?"

He wasn't sure what she meant. "I think so. Why?"

"They seem…sad to me. I mean, I understand why. I was just wondering if you thought…well, what do you think?"

"I think they're doing the best that they can."

"You seem better than they are."

"Tasha wasn't my daughter." He ran his fingertips along Natalie's leg. "Sure, I loved her. I miss her like crazy. But it isn't the same relationship. And I have Marie." He nuzzled her neck, taking a deep breath of her sugary and powdery scent. "And you." He kissed the soft spot below her ear, pleased when she melted and arched into him at the same time.

"I was just worried about them," she whispered.

"That's because you're a kind person." He traced his lips along her jaw.

She gripped his shoulders, all but climbing into his lap. "Do you think your dad liked my cookies?"

Owen chuckled, the heat and desire diving through him almost impossible to tame. "He ate six of them, Nat. So yeah, I think he liked them." He placed a kiss on each of her closed eyes. "You're a beautiful and caring person."

"Marie asked me if we were going to get married."

Owen pulled back, his eyes popping open. Natalie opened hers much slower, the sleepy, lazy quality of them sharpening the longer she looked at him. "What did you tell her?"

"I said I didn't know." She searched his face. "What would you have told her?"

A smile leaked across his face. "Sneaky question."

"It deserves an answer, don't you think?" She placed a

kiss too close to his earlobe to be friendly. He wasn't sure how to answer her—or Marie. He wasn't sure why he couldn't just propose now. Natalie spent more time at his house than her own.

But something—no, some*one*—held him back. "I'll talk to Marie," he said. "I don't want her to...I don't know what she's thinking or how she'll react." He cursed himself for not bringing it up with her *before* he'd started dating Natalie. Truth was, he didn't know how to parent an eight-year-old, didn't know what they understood and didn't, what they needed besides the obvious.

And then there was the whole sticky point of telling Natalie he loved her. It had taken him six months to tell Marie, and that love was inherent, parental. This love was in its infancy, and Owen wasn't even sure he was quite "in love" yet.

He knew he liked kissing her, so he did that until she told him she needed to get on home. He drove her home, drunk on the taste of her lips, the scent of her skin, the feel of her beside him.

"See you in the morning." She started to slide across the seat, but he touched her leg. She turned back to him and he kissed her again, taking it farther than he had before. She put one palm on his chest and gently pushed him back. "Owen."

"I don't want you to go."

Her dark eyes burned in the dim light, and he couldn't quite read them. "See you in the morning."

He let her go this time, not sure why he craved her so

THE COWBOY AND THE NANNY

much tonight. He felt vulnerable, and weak, and she made him feel stronger and better. By morning, the feelings he didn't understand had vanished, and when Natalie entered his house, he stayed in the kitchen entrance.

"Sorry about last night," he said, his voice low so as to not wake Marie. "I shouldn't have kissed you like that." He wanted to—and a lot more—but they weren't married, and he shouldn't compromise his standards—or hers—like that. He wouldn't.

"It's okay."

"It's not," he insisted. "Maybe you'll need to have a curfew or something." He was being serious, and he hoped she wouldn't get offended. "I mean, I want you to stay, and that's the real problem. It's me. Not you." Tar Baby left his food bowl and sat next to Owen, licking his chops as they both watched Natalie.

"Oh, it's me too." She tucked her hands in her pockets and stayed where she was. "So a curfew sounds great. And I can drive myself back and forth so you don't have to drive me home. I guess I usually do. Yesterday was just...different."

He nodded and turned back to the kitchen to gather his thermos, his lunch, and his wallet. Yesterday had been different, and not just because he'd gone too far with the kissing. "I'll get Marie from school today," he said. "I already sent her a text about it, so would you make sure she looks at her phone before school?"

"Yeah, of course. Why are you getting her?"

"I want to talk to her about us." He shoved his wallet in

his back pocket and his phone in his front one. "You can come over after dance if you want."

"Maybe," she said, a new awkwardness between them that Owen wanted to erase if only he knew how.

He dipped his hat in her direction. "See you later then." He moved into the living room, right into her personal space. "I sure like you, Natalie." He brushed his lips across hers for barely a moment and headed out the front door before she could say anything in return.

———

"Toby, that saddle is backward." Owen tamped down his rising frustration. Today marked the fifth week for this group of boys, and every one of them should know how to saddle a horse properly by now.

"Which one?" The tall, gangly boy glanced around like it was his first day at Silver Creek.

"The one on Bluebell. Hurry up and fix it. The girls will be here any minute." He turned to the other boys, who'd all finished their tasks correctly. "Davy, you and Kelton go get the guitar out of my truck. It's unlocked. Vinchenzo and Griff, will you go get us all some water?" The two boys nodded. "Kyle, you stay with me and Toby. All right, boys?"

"All right, Mister Carr," they said, and some of the tension that had been riding in his muscles since the previous night bled away. He watched Davy and Kelton start toward the end of the barn and disappear around it, where the parking lot was. The two hadn't gotten along when they'd first arrived, so Owen had paired them up and told them to figure things out.

"How's this, Mister Carr?" Toby panted as he jogged over. "Better?"

Owen pretended to inspect the saddle, even going so far as to pull on the straps to test the tightness. "You got it, Toby." He flashed him a quick smile. "Now come on, boys. I'm tired today, and we're gonna go sit down and have us a sing-in."

"A sing-in?" Kyle, the biggest boy in this batch, scoffed. "I don't sing, Owen."

"Well I do, and you can just listen."

He spotted the two boys he'd sent for water lugging it out of the cabin where he used to live. "Right there, boys," he called. "Just leave it on the porch."

Kelton came around the end of the barn, alone and in a dead sprint. "Owen!" He waved his arms, skidded to a stop, and pointed back the way he'd come. "Davy took your guitar and ran off!"

Owen reached for the radio on his belt at the same time he started running toward Kelton. "Which way did he go?" he called.

"North. He went north!"

Owen pressed the radio button at the same time he barked at the boys to gather on the porch of the cabin and stay put. "This is Owen Carr, at-risk counselor for unit thirteen. I have a runner," he said into the radio as he gained the corner of the barn. "David Thomas Yeates. I sent him with another boy to collect my guitar from my truck in the southwest parking lot. I was just informed that the boy took my guitar and ran north. I am arriving in the parking lot now."

"David Yeates," the secretary said over the radio. "Seventeen years old. Drug charges, and use of a weapon to injure or kill a small animal. Dark brown hair, brown eyes, stands at five-foot-nine-inches. Any known weapons?"

"Just the guitar that I know of," Owen said, scanning the area. He couldn't see anything but cars. The road leading up the canyon to the cabin community ran along this side of the parking lot, and across that—to the north—the trees started.

Thunder crashed overhead, and Owen called, "Davy, come on back now. It's gonna rain and you're gonna get real wet."

A quick movement in the trees across from him caught his eye. "He's across the street," Owen said quietly into the radio. "I repeat, he's left the parking lot and the Silver Creek facility and entered the woods on the north side of Canyon Road."

People chattered on the radio about the authorities being notified and personnel being moved, and Doctor Richards came on. "Owen, do you think you can get him by yourself?"

"Possibly." Owen's gut screamed at him to request backup. And he didn't ignore his gut. "But send someone over to stay with my other boys, and I'd like a hand with Davy too." He'd read the boy's file, just like he always did. He'd been in lots of fights at school, mixed up in drugs and girls. It wasn't until his mother had found the neighbor's dead cat that she sought help and Davy had ended up at Silver Creek.

"Davy," Owen tried again. "I'm not upset with you." His boots crunched on the gravel as he went up the bank to the road. "You don't even have a jacket." Work in the barn was often sweaty, even in the colder months. It hadn't snowed yet, but Owen knew what a Montana rainstorm looked like, and the sky was about to open.

Owen crossed the road and stood on the other side, scanning for movement as he searched his mind for what Davy had been wearing. Jeans and a brown sweatshirt. "Come on now, Davy. Tell me what's goin' on." He'd turned down the radio, but heard that the police had just arrived. Behind him, he heard the unmistakable footsteps of another person. He cast a quick glance over his shoulder and saw Trenton. Owen motioned for him to go further down the road, and Trenton complied.

"The police are here," Owen called. "I bet they brought their dogs. I'd hate for you to get hurt."

Davy stepped out from behind a tree, Owen's guitar held tightly in one hand. His expression stormed across the distance between them, and Owen stared right back. "I don't like horses," Davy yelled.

Thirty yards separated them, and Owen didn't take another step. "All right."

"And I don't like Kelton."

"I'll pair you up with someone else."

Davy looked at the guitar in his hand, and Owen's heart

squeezed. He'd recorded his album with that guitar, but a boy's life was worth more than a musical instrument. He searched, prayed, for the right thing to say.

"You want me to teach you how to play that thing?" he called into the wind.

Davy lifted his eyes back to Owen's. "Could you?"

"Of course." Owen went down the bank and crashed through the undergrowth. "You must not know who I am." Owen wove through the trees, keeping Davy in sight until they stood only a few yards apart. He hadn't planned on hiking that day, and his cowboy boots weren't fit for tromping through the woods. "I'm your counselor." Owen infused as much compassion into his voice as he could. "But I also recorded an album with that there guitar. The album went platinum, and one of my songs topped the country music charts."

Davy blinked at him and then the guitar, and back to him. "No way."

"Yes way. *Down on Your Luck?* Ever heard of it?" Owen chuckled, though he didn't feel settled or happy. "Of course you haven't. It was nine years ago. You'd have only been a little kid."

"I've always wanted to learn to play the guitar. My mom wouldn't pay for lessons."

Owen stepped forward and extended his hand toward the boy. "Good thing you came to Silver Creek then. Guitar lessons here are free." He silently thanked the Lord that the words were there. He hadn't thought of them himself;

wouldn't have dreamed of offering to teach Davy how to play the guitar at all.

Davy started to hold out the guitar for Owen to take, but he shook his head. "Davy, I don't care about the guitar. I care about *you*."

The teenager's chin shook, and Owen crossed the distance between them, taking the boy into his arms and holding him tight against his chest. "There you go." Davy cried, and Owen's guitar made a reverberating, discordant sound when it hit the ground.

CHAPTER 15

"*I* can't get Marie," Owen said to Natalie an hour later. "Something happened with one of my boys. Can you get her? Tell her I really wanted to be there, and I'll come get her at the studio as soon as I can?" He glanced over his shoulder to where Davy stood with Dr. Richards and two police officers.

It wasn't even lunch time yet. He probably could still get Marie, but Owen had a feeling his boys would need him. He felt stretched thin, even when Natalie said, "Of course, Owen. Is everything okay?"

He exhaled. "Everything *will* be okay. I have to go." He hung up and returned to Davy's side. He listened while Dr. Richards told him he'd have to call his mother, and explained that there wasn't anywhere to go after Silver Creek.

"Besides jail," an officer said. "I'm sure you don't want to go there."

Davy shook his head, his cheeks still tear-stained.

"Time to make different decisions then," the officer said, and then turned to Dr. Richards. "I don't think you need us for anything else."

Dr. Richards thanked them for coming so quickly, and they left. "Davy—" he began.

"I want to keep him with me," Owen interrupted. It was standard for the offending boy to be removed from the group, sometimes for several days. "I was just gonna sing with them until lunch. Maybe he can come over and meet with you after that."

Dr. Richards searched his face, and Owen silently pleaded with him to understand somehow. "Are you sure, Owen?"

"Absolutely sure," he said. "He's a good kid. Just got...mixed up."

Davy lifted his chin off his chest and stared at Owen, the disbelief plain to see.

"What about Kelton?"

"Kelton said nothing happened. Davy didn't touch him."

Dr. Richards sighed. "One o'clock, in my office. I want you, Kelton, and Davy to come together."

"Will do." Owen saluted as the director walked off. "You owe me," he whispered to Davy. "*And* I have to teach you how to play the guitar. I don't see what I'm gettin' out of any of this." He gave the boy a smile, and Davy actually returned it.

"I'm real sorry, Mister Carr."

"You *will* have to explain yourself," he said. "But I bought you a couple of hours." He swung back toward the barn. "Now, I left the other boys at my cabin. Let's go make sure they haven't ransacked the place."

———

Natalie exchanged a glance with one of Owen's boys. Davy he'd called himself when he'd "accidentally" run into her as she'd arrived with Marie. The teenager had gone to great lengths to get in touch with her—something Owen had told her the boys couldn't do when she'd asked—last week, and now he nodded toward the door.

She glanced at Owen, who seemed fully engaged with Marie and Ole Red, and followed Davy outside. He stood on the porch of the cabin several yards past the barn, and Nat made her steps slow and casual so she could just be pretending to walk somewhere if someone asked.

She knew Davy was the one who'd taken Owen's guitar and fled three weeks ago. She knew Owen had been giving the teenager guitar lessons ever since. She knew, because he'd been coming home later every Tuesday and Thursday.

"Davy," she said as she approached. "What is going on?"

"I just need your email address," he said, pulling out a phone Natalie knew he wasn't supposed to have. A benefit of her and Owen not kissing all the time—if there was one —was that he'd told her a lot about his job, his boys, the rules at Silver Creek.

"What for?" She glanced at the phone. "And where did you get that? If Owen sees you with—"

"Which is why you need to hurry." He flashed her a look of irritation. "Look, Owen's been teaching me how to play the guitar, right? Well, he's been singing a lot lately, and he's been teaching us one of his songs. I asked him if I could record it, and he sort of freaked out, but then Kyle said he could cut it and make it sound professional, and we all begged him, and he brought in the equipment. Computer, microphone, the whole works." He glanced toward the barn.

"And I talked to Doctor Richards, who said I could email you the file. But I don't want Owen to know, and I just need your email address."

Still confused, but following along well enough, Natalie gave him her email address. His thumbs moved feverishly as she asked, "What do you expect me to do with it?"

He tapped a final time and shoved the phone inside his coat. "I don't know. I just thought you'd want to hear it." He grinned at her as he moved down from the shadowy porch. "Owen says it's about you."

Her phone chimed as Davy hurried back into the barn. Natalie sat down on the steps of the cabin where Owen said he usually sat with the boys while he played his guitar. Since they'd started dating, she hadn't heard him play or sing once. But she'd seen the guitar at his house, sometimes in the kitchen, and sometimes the living room. He obviously picked it up from time to time.

The email from Davy sat in her inbox, but she hesitated to open it. She'd brought Marie to Silver Creek early tonight, because she was headed to Wyoming. Julie was expecting her by noon tomorrow for Thanksgiving dinner, and if she could get out of the mountains and into Butte, her drive tomorrow would be much easier.

Feeling brave and trying to act like it, she opened the email. No message. No subject. Just an mp4 file. She touched it and her phone started to download it. She stood suddenly, not wanting to hear Owen's feelings for her portrayed in a song he'd only sung for six teenage boys. Not her. He hadn't even mentioned that he was still composing music and lyrics, still singing the way he used to.

Was he not satisfied with his life in Gold Valley? Did he want to return to Nashville and try for a career in country music again? The fact that she didn't know—hadn't even thought to ask him—grated against her nerves.

She pushed the power button on her phone and it went dark. She needed to get on the road if she was going to get ahead of the storm. Owen and Marie were leaving for Idaho Falls the following morning, their drive three hours shorter than hers. And Owen didn't worry about driving in a storm in his truck.

Glancing at the barn, she decided she'd listen to the song in the car, a safe distance from Owen and after telling him goodbye for the weekend. He appeared in the barn doorway when she was about fifteen feet from it.

"Hey, gorgeous," he said. "I thought you'd left without sayin' goodbye."

She pushed a smile to her lips. "I wouldn't do that."

He received her into his embrace and she pressed her face to his neck and got a noseful of cologne, and musk, and horse. She cupped his face in her hands and kissed him.

"Mm." He kept his eyes closed after she broke their connection, a slow smile making him even more handsome. "That was nice. I think someone's gonna miss me." He chuckled and she smiled at him with all the emotion she could muster.

"I think someone will," she said. "I've never seen Ole Red all pouty like that." She danced out of his arms at his protest and squealed when he grabbed her by the arm and twirled her back into his chest.

His amusement faded as he gazed down at her. "I will miss you, Natalie." He pressed his lips to hers again, the intensity in his kiss matching what she'd poured into hers a few moments ago.

She stroked her fingers down the side of his face, over his beard, and along the back of his neck. "Owen, I think I might be in love with you."

His navy eyes sparked, but he didn't open his mouth and repeat the sentiment back to her. Her heart flopped around in her chest like it was choking, gasping.

"You let me know when you know for sure, all right sweetheart?"

"How are you feeling about us?" she asked, something she'd never done in high school. She'd let him kiss her, and hold her hand, and make her promises without knowing how he really felt. She'd told herself that his actions spoke louder than words, but once he'd finally told her he loved her, everything had changed.

"I'm wild about you," he whispered. "I feel great about us."

She pressed into him, leaning up on her tiptoes. "Can I tell my family that you'll be joining me for Christmas? Are you feeling that great about us?"

"I am, sweetheart." He glanced over his shoulder and fell away from her. When she checked the doorway, she didn't see anyone. "Has Marie said anything else to you?"

He'd spoken to her a few weeks ago, a couple of days after the incident with Davy. She was eight, but she knew Natalie was always at Owen's, holding her uncle's hand, and that they were dating.

Natalie hadn't been present in the conversation, but Owen said he explained that dating was a way to get to know someone. Get to know someone well enough to know if you wanted to marry them. When Marie had asked him if he was going to marry Natalie, he'd said he didn't know. He'd asked her if they should get married, and Marie had asked if she'd have to call Natalie mom.

That, combined with his opinion that he'd pushed too far physically, and he'd backed off over the past few weeks. Sure, she still saw him most mornings and evenings. They still held hands, and ate dinner together, and cuddled on the couch. But there was far less kissing, and definitely nothing as passionate as that night she'd eaten dinner with his parents.

"Nat?"

She swung her attention back to him. "No, Marie hasn't said anything else to me."

"Me either." He exhaled. "I'll talk to her on the way to Idaho Falls. Sort of see how she's feeling."

Natalie nodded, but what she really wanted to know was how Owen was feeling. She didn't think he'd use his niece as a reason why they couldn't get married, but the wicked thought lingered in her mind as she walked back to her car alone.

She didn't make it out of the parking lot before plugging in the headphone jack to her phone and opening the music file Davy had sent her. The sound of Owen's guitar playing was unique and beautiful, and Natalie closed her eyes and took a deep breath as she basked in the quality of it.

When he started singing, tears came to her eyes.

> *I haven't seen you in a decade*
> *But you're just as I remember*
> *That quick smile*
> *Those deep, dark eyes*
> *The scent of lemons and lavender*
> *My ultimate prize.*
>
> *If only I could say I'm sorry the right way*
> *If only we could start over in just one day*
> *But I know you need answers I can't give you*
> *Hopefully we'll find a way to start anew.*

She wasn't sure what Owen wanted when it came to his music, but it felt wrong to rob the world of his talent, his voice, his influence. And she knew she'd be a bit delayed from going to Wyoming.

She flipped the car into drive and headed back to his

house, thanking the stars and the Lord that he never locked his front door. She felt like an intruder, though she'd entered his house a hundred times without knocking and without him there.

His laptop sat on the nightstand in his bedroom, and she perched on the edge of his bed as she opened his Internet browser. It hadn't been closed, and several windows popped up. Being careful not to close any, she found his email.

He hadn't been as forthcoming about his life in Nashville as he'd been about his job at Silver Creek, but she knew the name of his record company. She typed *Universal Music* and two email addresses popped up. She put them both into her phone, deleted the evidence of her snooping, slapped the laptop closed, and scurried out of his house.

She made it past the city limits before her heart stopped thumping like a drum, before she pulled over and prepared the email. She let them know who she was and how she got the track, then she attached the song to the email, her heart once again tangoing in her chest.

Leaning her head against the rest behind her, she prayed, *Should I do this?*

She wasn't sure if it was God or herself that whispered, "Do it." She relied on her faith as she sent the email zipping from Montana to Nashville.

CHAPTER 16

N atalie pulled into her sister's ranch-style house a full twenty minutes early. She hadn't heard anything from Owen besides a *We're on our way! See you Sunday night* text. Nothing about his laptop being broken into or anything.

She'd been coaching herself for the past four hours to keep him to herself. Surely her mother and her sister would ask if she was seeing anyone. Despite the fact that she hadn't dated a man since her marriage had ended, they asked every time one of them spoke to her. She'd confessed to Julie last year that she just didn't think she was the marrying type.

Bracing herself for the crazy that embodied her older sister, Natalie knocked and entered the house. "Hello?"

A squeal erupted from the kitchen, and Julie spilled from it, her dark hair flying around her face as she came to meet Natalie. "You're here, you're here!" Julie laughed and hugged

Natalie, who felt so welcome and accepted with only four words.

"How are Mom and Dad?" Natalie asked quietly.

"Oh, you know." Julie stepped back and smoothed her hair. One of her hands bore the evidence of flour and her apron said that a massacre waited in the kitchen. "They're Mom and Dad."

"So Dad's grumpy and Mom's overly chipper?"

Julie's peal of laughter actually hurt Natalie's eardrums. "Yes, like that. Now come help me in the kitchen. I need you to make the gravy and then we'll be ready."

Natalie gasped at the state of the kitchen. Dishes were stacked on every available surface as the sink was filled to capacity. A large, browned turkey sat next to a pot covered with a tea towel. A bowl with rolls waited next to that, and she moved another covered pot next to those.

"I told Dad I needed him to carve the turkey, but he said it was too hot. So now we're waiting for it to cool." She gave Natalie an annoyed stare as she picked up a wooden spoon. "Meanwhile, the potatoes, stuffing, corn, and rolls are going to get stone cold." She flicked the wooden spoon toward the stove and drops went flying. "Gravy right there. Work your magic."

She wielded a whisk like a wand and had the gravy ready in no time flat. Unfortunately, her father insisted on having a "family talk," where he spoke about gratitude and all they had to be thankful for.

Natalie smiled and got emotional, especially since this year had started out cloaked in bleakness and had only started to look up come summer. But she wouldn't be saying that when it came her turn to name something she was grateful for this year.

Luckily, Julie rambled on about her job and her friends and the homeless shelter where she volunteered by sorting clothes and serving soup.

"Natalie," her father prompted. All she wanted to do was eat, but the turkey sat on the counter, un-carved, the side dishes all covered in the hopes of keeping them warm until her father deemed them ready to eat.

"I'm grateful for a new job that's allowed me to live a little easier."

Her mother's eyes squinted. "You didn't mention a new job."

"Yeah." Natalie cleared her throat. "I've been a nanny since July."

"A nanny?" Julie piped up. No one had asked her a bunch of follow-up questions. Maybe Natalie should've gone on and on about her cooking classes and the little girls she taught to dance. Sure, she was grateful for them too. But it all came back to Owen this year. Without him, she'd have lost her car in August.

"Yes, a nanny."

"For who?"

"An eight-year-old little girl. Her dad works early in the morning and late at night. I help in the morning and the evening. He even pays me to cook dinner, and I do a little housework." She took a quick breath and forged on as she saw her mom preparing to ask another question. "It's nice, because it doesn't interfere with my ballet classes, so I've been able to have the extra income I need and still keep teaching dance, which I love."

She glanced at her father, pleading for him to move to Mom. They'd always shared a special connection, and he said, "Heather, what about you? What are you grateful for this year?"

The conversation moved on, thankfully, but Natalie knew it was only the first of many bullets she'd need to dodge before this weekend ended. She wondered how long she could go without telling Julie or her mother that she was the nanny for Owen Carr's new daughter.

That night, sequestered in the guest room with the door closed, she opened her email, a twitch of discomfort in her stomach that had nothing to do with the double scoop of mashed potatoes and the two pieces of pecan pie—with ice cream—she'd consumed that day.

"They haven't answered in one day," she muttered as she scanned the various Black Friday emails. "Over a holiday."

Sure enough, they hadn't. She had no idea if Jim or Amy still worked at the Universal Music Group. Owen had left the country music scene seven years ago. She kept her hope close to her heart, especially since the emails hadn't bounced back as undeliverable.

Happy Thanksgiving, she sent to Owen, along with three turkey emoticons. She pressed her phone to her chest as she waited for him to answer. Then she realized that it was past ten, and with the early hour at which he rose, he'd likely already gone to bed.

Sure enough, she didn't hear from him, though she stayed up for another half an hour, waiting. During that time, her thoughts ran from one side of her mind to the other, each time inventing a new reason why he wasn't able to tell her he loved her.

Maybe he didn't love her.

Maybe he just needed more time.

Maybe he didn't want to mix business with pleasure.

Maybe, maybe, maybe.

She wasn't sure what to think, and she needed to talk to Owen about his music before she did anything else with him. Determined in her new plan, she was finally able to sleep.

————

Owen wanted to stop by Natalie's when he got back into town on Sunday afternoon, but Marie had fallen asleep on the seat next to him. He thought it best to just head on home and text her. She should've made it home much earlier than him, because the drive from Butte was only four hours.

You home? he texted after he'd carried Marie into her bedroom and tucked her in. She'd had a great time in Idaho Falls, where a skimming of snow had dusted the ground. Henry's two brothers had been in town too, and Marie had enjoyed playing with her cousins.

A pang of regret stung Owen's heart as he watched her sleep. Maybe he should move to Idaho, where Marie would have family her own age, other little girls to play with instead of a grown woman and a cowboy who worked too much.

He'd been thinking about it but hadn't quite arrived at a decision yet. He needed to talk to Natalie. Needed to really have a grown-up, intelligent discussion with her about life, and Marie, and what was best for all of them.

He froze in the process of kicking off his boots. Even when his phone chimed—probably a text from Nat—he didn't move.

"You're planning a future with her." His voice seemed to echo through his quiet house. "You want what's best for everyone. You're in love with Natalie."

And he knew in that moment that he had fallen in love with her again. All the way, head-over-heels in love with her.

His phone sounded again, launching him into motion. Natalie had responded. Her first text made his heart race: *I'm home and would love to see you.*

Her second made it fall to his boots, where it continued to freak out: *We need to talk.*

Though he agreed, and he had some topics of his own he wanted to address, nothing good ever came from when a woman said, "We need to talk."

Marie fell asleep in the truck. I need to grab Tar Baby from the neighbor, and then I'll just be at home. Come on over anytime.

Tar Baby was excited to see him, and Owen scrubbed him behind the ears and paid the teenager he'd asked to take the dog. Back at home, Owen lay down on the couch, beyond grateful and glad to be home. He was too much of a homebody to want to travel the world, as his five-year stint in Nashville had taught him.

He began to hum the song he'd written last month. His boys had inspired him, especially Davy. Working with someone else on his music was intoxicating, and something Owen hadn't even realized he missed doing. Sure, he still loved to play the guitar and sing, and he did those things all the time. But he hadn't composed a song in years.

Already, new lyrics ran through his mind, and he found himself inspired by the simplest things, the way he used to be when he was actively trying to write songs. Maybe he could write songs from Montana. He knew most artists didn't compose their own music—it was something that had set him apart as more than a singer.

"Owen?"

He sat up straight up, swiping his cowboy hat off in the same motion. He couldn't help the smile on his face or the way his heart beat against the back of his throat. "Hey."

He stood to meet her, hugging her tight and then kissing her like it was the first time all over again. "I missed you," he murmured, swaying with her as she pressed her cheek to his chest.

"How was Idaho Falls?"

"You know, it was really amazing. Henry's parents are good people. His brothers were there with their families." His hands on her back fisted and released. "It's actually something I want to talk to you about."

"What is?"

"Moving to Idaho Falls."

She jerked out of his arms. "Moving to Idaho Falls?" Her eyebrows stretched so high, they nearly reached her hairline. "What are you talking about?"

"Marie has two additional uncles in Idaho Falls. They have children her age. Children she could play with." He didn't tell her she wasn't the ideal playmate or confess about his guilt for working so much, for often putting his boys first.

"Well, I—" She blinked and paced away from him. "I don't know what to say right off the top of my head."

"Just something to think about," he said. "It's not like I'd be moving right away." He was careful not to say "we." He'd made that mistake before, grouping them together in his plans.

"I have something for you to think about too," she said. "Well, not really, but more of a question."

"All right."

"Do you ever think about giving country music a second try? Like, do you want to try again for another album?"

He wasn't sure where the question had come from, but it was obvious it weighed heavily on Natalie. "I don't know," he said honestly. "I don't want to live in Nashville again, I know that. But…."

She waited for the time it took to breathe a couple of times before saying, "But what?"

"But I've been writing songs again, and I kinda want to keep doing it," he blurted. "But then I think of how demanding my job already is, and how I'm already neglecting Marie, and I wonder how I can even consider trying to add song-writing to my already full plate." He sighed and gestured for her to come to him. She complied, wrapping her long arms around his back and holding all his questions, all his confusion, inside.

"Something to think about," she said. "That's all."

"That's all," he repeated, his mind whirring now when it had just been churning before.

CHAPTER 17

Owen did a lot of thinking over the next couple of weeks. He talked to Natalie, and asked her questions, and they brainstormed about Marie and Idaho Falls. When she'd asked what he would do for a living, he'd hemmed and hawed until he finally admitted he didn't actually have to work.

She'd paused in stirring the Alfredo sauce she'd been making. "You don't have to work at all?"

"Not for money, no."

She blinked and stared, stared and blinked. "You haven't —you've been back in Gold Valley for seven years."

"Yeah."

"And you don't have to work." At least she'd stopped asking, but the statement sounded so much worse.

"I still get money every quarter from the record label," he said. "My album still sells, and my single does...decently well."

"Decently well?" She laughed and turned back to her sauce. She whisked furiously, muttering under her breath. When he'd asked what was wrong, she said the sauce had started to burn, that was all.

But it wasn't all. His money obviously bothered Natalie for some reason. He hadn't asked her why yet.

In the end, he'd decided not to move to Idaho Falls. With that decision made, he'd been talking more and more about songwriting and if he could collaborate remotely. He didn't know, and he hadn't dared use any of his former contacts in the industry to find out. He hadn't fully decided that he wanted to return to country music, even just to dip his toes into the song-writing side of it.

During his lunch break, he saw that Natalie had called. He dialed her back, a tad nervous that she'd called when she usually texted, when she knew he wouldn't be able to answer right away.

"Hey," he said when she picked up. "What's goin' on?"

"My mother wants me to come home for Christmas. I was wondering if you and Marie would come with me. Remember we talked about it a while ago?"

"I remember." He looked off into the distance, weighing his options. "Natalie, do I need to tell you right now?"

"She wants to know, and I couldn't think of a reason not to tell her, but I made something up about someone else calling and got off the line. I said I'd call her back and let her know."

"All right." He exhaled. "I was hopin' to talk to you in person about this, but—"

"Owen," her voice carried a heavy dose of warning.

"I love you," he said, his voice carrying in the winter air. "For a while there, I wasn't sure, and I felt trapped, caught between the reins. But now I know. I'm in love with you." He chuckled. "So yeah, I think Marie and I should come to Wyoming with you for Christmas."

The silence on the other end of the line felt bottomless. Sounded deafening. Consumed him whole.

"Nat?" he asked. "Did you hear me?"

"I heard you," she whispered. "I'm just sort of stunned."

"Why's that?" He frowned. "You're stunned that I'm in love with you?" He wasn't sure how to feel, but he knew he didn't like the pinch in his chest.

"A little bit, yeah," she said. "Even more so that you told me over the phone."

"I didn't want you to think I was going to go to Wyoming without being fully committed to you."

"Fully committed?" Her voice strayed into a higher octave, and he realized what that probably translated to in her ears. "What does that mean?"

"It means I love you, and I wanted you to know before we go visit your family. That's all."

"All right," she said, and she sounded a lot like him when he said those words.

He smiled and said, "I have to go, Nat. See you tonight?"

"After hearing what I just heard, I'm having a hard time not coming over there right now."

"You can come," he said.

She giggled. "Oh, I don't think so. I'm not into kissing in front of teenagers."

He laughed, the sound bouncing up to the cloudy sky and filling his world with joy. He'd barely hung up when his phone rang again. He didn't recognize the number, but that didn't mean much. People had numbers from all over these days.

He swiped the call on. "Hello?"

"Is this Owen Carr?"

"Sure is." He gave up on eating during lunch today and wondered when he'd be able to stuff a few bites of sandwich into his mouth.

"Owen, this is Jim Guthrie from Universal Music Group. How are you?"

How was he? *Jim Guthrie* echoed through his mind. Why in the world was Jim Guthrie—the vice-president of the Universal Music Group—calling *him*?

"Fine, I guess." He couldn't help asking, "Why are you calling, Jim?"

"We got your new track, Owen, and it's your best work. Another number one hit."

Owen had no idea what to say. "I'm sorry, sir, but I have no idea what you're talking about."

"The new track your manager sent us a couple of weeks ago."

Icy fingers reached down his throat. "My manager?"

"Yeah, a woman named Natalie Ringold. Listen, Owen, she sent us the track, and we all love it. When can you get down to Nashville?"

Never, he wanted to say. He had no desire to return to Nashville, even for a meeting. *Settle down,* he told himself as if he were a restless horse. He took a deep breath, and said, "Not until the new year. Hey, Jim, can you send me a copy of the track? I just want to make sure Natalie sent you the right one."

"Sure thing, Owen. Coming your way. Let's set something up for January."

"I'll have my manager call you," he said and hung up before he went completely berserk. He turned in a circle, not quite sure where to look or what to do or anything. He felt like his whole world had been put in a blender and liquefied.

He got a text from Jim, with an attachment. An attachment that when Owen tapped it and it started to play, featured his voice and his fingers strumming the guitar. As he listened to the song he'd written and practiced on Sunday mornings—the song he'd written about Natalie and second chances—his emotions clashed. Pride at the flawless lyrics. Horror that she'd listened to this without his knowledge.

How in the world had Natalie gotten that? He'd never even told her about it until two weeks ago, and he still hadn't played it for her.

Boys started streaming out of the cafeteria, and everything aligned in Owen's head. "Davy!" he called as he spotted his boys peeling off and heading toward the barn. Owen started after them, fire in every step. "Davy, I need to talk to you right this second."

———

Natalie glanced up as the wind shook the window right in its frame. The storm that had been predicted had arrived, and she hoped Owen would soon too. She hated the thought of him being outside in the darkness while it snowed and snowed and snowed, as this storm was predicted to do.

He had the next three days off, and a content smile floated across her face as she imagined a lazy weekend with him—the man who'd just told her he loved her.

She didn't hear anything, but when Tar Baby perked up from his spot at the end of the counter, she glanced toward the front door. Sure enough, Owen blew through it a few seconds later.

He managed to trap out the cold, and wind, and snow in a matter of moments. He brushed the wetness from his jacket and shook out his hat. He removed them both and hung them by the door. He said nothing, and a tremor rattled through Natalie's ribcage.

"You made it," she said to fill the silence. "I have chili on, and the cornbread will be done in ten minutes."

He didn't look at her; didn't acknowledge her. She paused in her movement to get bowls from the cupboard. Owen bent down and kissed the top of Marie's head, murmuring something to her. She looked up at him and said, "Right now?"

"Yes, please."

"All right," she said in the same western drawl Owen

used, which made a flood of adoration flow through Natalie for the pair of them. Marie left the TV on, where she'd been watching a cooking show Natalie had told her about, and went down the hall to her bedroom. She didn't look at Natalie either.

"What's wrong?" she asked as soon as the door snicked closed.

"What's wrong?" Owen kept perfectly still in his spot in the living room. He looked as fierce and dangerous as the blizzard billowing, blowing, blustering beyond the window.

"Bad day at work?"

"It was actually pretty great. My boys are doing well, getting excited for Christmas. They're gearing up to go home in a couple of weeks. I call my girlfriend and tell her I love her."

He didn't soften, didn't yield. She wanted to rush into his arms, declare her undying love for him too, kiss him until her lips felt bruised, but the combative way he stood apart from her screamed angry, and she stayed in the kitchen with the counter and the dog between them.

"Then what happened?" she asked.

"Jim Guthrie called."

Natalie's blood turned to ice. A river of ice that flowed like a glacier, moving so slowly and choking near her heart. "Oh."

"*You* sent him a track I'd recorded with my boys." He stalked one step closer. "You had no right to do that."

"It's a beautiful song, Owen. When I heard it, I knew the world needed to experience it too."

"That's not your decision to make." He glowered at her.

"Did you talk to Davy?" she asked, lifting her chin. "He's the one who gave it to me. Said all the boys wanted to send it in. I'm just the one who could actually do it, you know, because they're *juvenile delinquents*."

Owen's anger visibly deflated, and that grated grated grated at Natalie. She realized in that moment that he loved his boys unconditionally. "Did you turn all cold with him?" she asked, her voice strangely robotic.

"I spoke with him."

"In this angry, condescending tone? With barely suppressed fury in every line of your face?" She shook her head and turned away, her insides shaking and quaking. "I doubt it."

"What does that mean?"

She faced him again, employing her bravery, her determination. "It means, *Mister Carr*, that you save your best self for those boys. You give *them* every opportunity to please you, and you forgive *them* easily. Then when you get home, you're too tired—emotionally and physically—to do much more than check homework and fall asleep on the couch." Her chest rose and fell, rose and fell, rapidly, and she couldn't get a decent breath.

His navy eyes darkened and the flush in his face was no longer from the cold. "That is not true."

She folded her arms. "Then tell me how the conversation went with Davy."

When Owen balked, tears sprang to Natalie's eyes. She hadn't wanted to be right, not this time. "That's what I thought." She glanced at the oven. "Cornbread has four minutes left, and I made a compound herb butter. It's in the fridge." She walked into the living room, her skin itching beneath her sweater and along her neck. He didn't try to stop her as she calmly shrugged into her coat and wrapped a scarf around her neck.

He didn't try to stop her as she stuffed a hat on her head and shoved her hands into her gloves.

He didn't try to stop her when she wrenched open his front door and stepped into the storm.

He simply didn't try to stop her, the way she would've tried to stop him from going to Nashville without her all those years ago.

CHAPTER 18

$\mathcal{N}$atalie made it home through a sheer miracle and the grace of God. She sat in her garage, the car off and the door behind her closed, the only way she felt like no one would hear her sobs.

She cried until she felt dried out, and the pain still existed. She wondered if she'd have to live with this dull ache in her chest for the rest of her life. She'd felt like this before. First, when Owen had left when they were eighteen-years-old. Second, when she'd told Jeremiah she wanted a divorce.

Both of those aches felt miniscule in comparison to this one. This one went on and on, radiating a jolt down to her toes and out to her fingers every few seconds.

Eventually, the cold settled in her bones and she had to go into the house. Not long ago, she'd loved coming home to the peace and quiet of her home. She'd felt comfortable there, alone, secluded, isolated behind the walls where she could dance and cook and simply be herself.

But now that she'd had a taste of family life, of interacting with a child she loved, and making dinner for the man she loved, she couldn't fathom being happy by herself. She'd done what Pastor Palmer had suggested, had looked to something new to focus on, had been feeding her faith.

So why did she feel completely abandoned, both by Owen and by God? Her tears started afresh and as she looked at the thermostat, she realized it was nearly as cold inside as out. Her teeth chattered as she jammed her finger on the button to up the temperature.

Nothing happened.

"Great," she said through her tears. She inhaled and wiped her face. She'd only turned on one light in the kitchen after she'd entered the house, and as she looked around now, everything in her life stood out in contrast.

Owen's house had been full of life, and light, and love. Hers was dark and cold, with a furnace that had chosen to malfunction during a December blizzard.

He made her laugh with abandon, and all she wanted to do now was leave this life in Gold Valley. She'd tried, she honestly had. But she hated the winter, and she could teach dance in any city in the country. Didn't have to be here.

She moved to the couch and pulled a blanket around her shoulders, really examining herself. *Why did you stay in Gold Valley after Mom and Dad left?*

She knew why: Owen Carr.

She'd never lost hope for them—until tonight.

What do you need to be happy?

Again, the answer was easy: Owen Carr.

But the familiar fear and worry engulfed her and she lay down, the tears still flowing across her face. Owen already had a lot in his life. A darling niece. A fulfilling, yet demanding, job. Loads of money.

He didn't *need* Natalie the way she needed him. "What do I do now?" she whispered into the chilly, gray house.

Can't stay here, her mind whispered back. *Too cold.*

She thought of when Owen had left. She'd gone into shock, unable to do much more than breathe. Her father had been there, bringing her food and telling her to get out of the house, go do something.

"Come on now, Nat," he says, holding a bottle of water and placing a plate on the nightstand next to where she lies on the bed. "You have to eat something."

She glances at him, promises she will, but after he leaves, she just keeps staring out the window. Finally, in the dead of night, when everyone sleeps, Nat leaves the house and wanders to the water tower.

She climbs to the top and looks out over the sleeping town of Gold Valley. She hates this town, hates that Owen abandoned her here. Fierce fury foams inside her, and she releases a scream.

Then she's sobbing and storming and saying things about Owen she hopes she won't remember later. But at least she doesn't feel so tight inside anymore. At least she doesn't feel like her next breath will be the one that fills her too full and will cause her to explode.

She marches home and makes herself a full meal. When her father leans against the wall, she apologizes for waking him. He says it's okay and settles at the kitchen counter to watch her cook.

"Feeling better?" he asks.

She's not but she does feel different, so she says, "Yes."

He pats her shoulder, embraces her tight. "There will be other boys, Nat."

She agrees because that's what her father expects. He wanders down the hall and back to bed, and she looks over the spread she made to eat.

She walks away without taking a bite.

Her dad wasn't here now, but the memory was enough to get her off the couch. She walked on wooden legs, but she walked. She packed a bag, and then another. She could stay at the hotel in town tonight and start for Wyoming in the morning. Maybe, if the snow wasn't too bad. Maybe, if they cleared the roads through the mountain pass. Maybe, if Owen didn't call and tell her he was sorry, that he loved her, and to please come back so they could talk.

But the fact that she'd left his house a half an hour ago and he hadn't so much as texted made her think that he wouldn't. She'd never seen him so angry. She actually didn't know the calm, cool, collected Owen could get that angry.

Over a stupid country song, she thought. She shook her head. She'd never imagined he'd react the way he had. Sure, she thought he might be frustrated with her, but those fears had fled when she'd asked him if he wanted to return to a country music career and he'd admitted that he wanted to be a song-writer.

After that, she'd relaxed. She thought he'd be thrilled she'd made the first move, opened the first door.

She picked up her suitcases and left without a backward glance. It took three times as long to get downtown, what with the wind whipping the snow sideways. As she checked in, she realized how isolated she'd become. She'd been spending so much time with Marie and Owen that she didn't feel comfortable asking Stephanie or any of her other friends if she could stay with them for one night.

Doesn't matter, she told herself as she handed over her debit card. *Because of Owen, you have enough money to stay in a hotel.*

Everything came back to Owen. It always had.

And she was really, really tired of that.

———

Owen turned off the timer on the oven. He wasn't sure how long it had been beeping, but the cornbread seemed a bit overbrowned. He didn't get out the compound butter. Didn't even know what that was. Didn't know what to do now.

He only fed Marie when she came down the hall and asked where Nat had gone. "She left," Owen said, because she had.

197

He couldn't believe he'd just let her leave. Let her leave without saying a single thing to her. Let her leave in the storm that raged across the countryside. Let her leave him and Marie.

Her words swirled through her head, batted against his brain, the same way the wind whipped and banged against his windows.

Marie had tugged on his sleeve to get him to step away from the sliding glass door, where he stared into the darkness. "Uncle Owen?" she asked. "Is she coming back? She said chili was her favorite."

Owen hadn't known how to answer, and his voice seemed to be stuck on mute anyhow. Marie had eventually settled down and eaten. She'd gone down the hall to do her homework. She'd brought it back for him to check. She'd put herself to bed.

All of it testified to Owen how much she didn't really need him. All this time, he'd been pretending she did, when the truth was, Marie had saved him. Saved him from looking and feeling as empty and hollow as his parents did.

Once Natalie had rejoined his life, everything in Owen's existence had brightened. He'd been kinder to his boys, more understanding, because of Natalie. She made him happier, and that bled into everything he did—including his music. He'd only written that song because of her. How could he be so angry with her for sending it in?

And the better question was: Why hadn't he been that furious with Davy or Kyle, the two boys who had hatched the plan to get the song to Natalie so she could send it to Nashville?

He didn't have an answer for either of his questions.

He couldn't leave during a blizzard to go find her and try to apologize.

So he did the next best thing. He swallowed his pride and picked up his phone.

———

Owen woke on Saturday morning, a painful kink in his neck because he'd slept on the couch. His phone rested on his chest because he kept checking it every few seconds to make sure he didn't miss a call or message from Natalie. He still hadn't.

He groaned as he sat up and saw a ray of sunshine through the sliding glass door. He couldn't believe he'd slept past five a.m., but given the circumstances of the previous evening, he felt as if he hadn't slept at all.

A dog barked, and he looked for Tar Baby. A childish squeal followed, and Owen stood and walked over to the door.

Marie had gotten dressed and taken Tar Baby into the backyard. They ran and played, and even through the turmoil in Owen's life, he smiled at the two of them. He called Natalie again, and left another message similar to the previous three he'd left last night.

"I'm real sorry, sweetheart," he said. "Please forgive me. Call me and tell me where to meet you. I'll be there." He exhaled, not sure what else to say to get her to call him. "I love you," he tacked on and hung up.

He squeezed his phone until he felt it give a little. After setting it on the counter, he opened the sliding glass door. "Marie," he called. Tar Baby spun and looked at him, the dog's tongue lolling out of the side of his mouth. "I'm gonna go shower. Then we're gonna go get breakfast, all right?"

"All right." She gathered another handful of snow and packed it into a ball.

Owen set a pot of coffee to brew and hurried down the hall to shower. His morning plans definitely included breakfast, but he'd be stopping by Natalie's first. If there was anything he could do to nudge her toward forgiving him, it would be bacon.

Forty-five minutes later, he sat in his truck in the street outside Natalie's house. The driveway and sidewalk hadn't been touched, and the two feet of snow that had fallen during the night glittered in the bright sun.

"Think she's home?" Marie asked as she peered toward the front door. "Did you call her?"

"I've called her," he said quietly. "And no, I don't think she's home." He wasn't sure how he knew, only that he did.

"Maybe you should go check." Marie turned her innocent eyes on him.

"All right." Owen unbuckled his seat belt and sloshed through the snow to Natalie's front step. He knocked and rang the doorbell. He called, "Nat, it's Owen." He opened her screen door and tried the front door, fully expecting it to be locked. It was.

He turned back to Marie and lifted his hands in an "I don't know," gesture. She pointed to the garage. So Owen slogged over there, the snow pushing up his jeans all the way to his knees. He knew the code, and he got the door open.

Her car was gone.

His heart turned to stone, and all he could do was stare at the empty space where her car should be. That space grew and expanded inside his chest, leaving him scrubbed out and stinging. He got himself to walk to the door leading to the house, which thankfully wasn't locked.

His breath billowed in front of him in a white cloud, even inside the house. No wonder Nat wasn't here. The tiniest balloon of hope began to fill within him. Her furnace had gone out, that's why she wasn't here. She hadn't left town. She'd simply gone to a hotel.

And since Gold Valley only had one hotel, Owen knew exactly where to go.

CHAPTER 19

"What do you mean, you can't tell me?" Owen leaned his full weight into the counter at the hotel, where Dahlia Carter stood. He'd gone to high school with her, knew her family. They'd owned this hotel for generations.

"I mean, I can't tell you, Owen." She only looked the slightest bit nervous. "It's hotel policy."

"You can't tell me if Natalie Ringold stayed here last night?"

"I can't." Something in her eyes told him she was lying.

"I don't think that's hotel policy," he pressed.

"Would you like me to call my father?"

"Yes, I would." But Owen really didn't want to waste the time. He needed to know if Natalie had been here. For some reason, it mattered. If she'd stayed in a hotel, he assumed her next step would be to leave town. But if she'd stayed with a friend, she'd probably meet the furnace repairman this morning to get her house back in order.

Dahlia hung up. "My father says we can't tell you." She gave him a sympathetic smile. "I'm sorry, Owen."

"It's okay." Owen turned away, frustrated but not hopeless. He'd fix Natalie's furnace, and he'd call her until she picked up the blasted phone.

By lunchtime, he and Marie had eaten breakfast, and he'd identified the problem with Natalie's furnace. Marie had been sitting in a patch of sunlight that hit Nat's couch, a blanket tucked around her body.

"Baby doll," he said. "I have to run to the hardware store. I'll grab us some sandwiches, okay? Will you be okay here?"

"Maybe I can wait at our house." She kicked the blanket off. "Tar Baby's there, and he'll help me not to be scared."

"You can just come with me," Owen said. "That's fine too."

"I want some of Nat's chili."

He tousled her messy hair, thinking Natalie would've braided it into a crown instead of allowing Marie to walk around looking homeless. "All right. Let's go back to our place."

Once he had Marie set up with a warm bowl of chili, Tar Baby begging at her side, he headed over to the hardware store for the parts he needed. He had the right filter and the appropriate fuses when he spotted Maureen Baldwin, the activity director at the church.

"Maureen." He practically rammed his cart into a display of paint trays in his haste to turn toward her. He approached her, taking in her curious expression. "Hey, Miss Baldwin," he started again. "I'm wondering if you've heard from Natalie. Will she be in her cooking classes this week?"

The brown-haired woman blinked. "Why, no, Owen. I spoke to her this morning. She said something had come up."

Owen's heart skyrocketed, though the information still didn't tell him where she'd gone. "Oh, that's too bad," he said. "Marie loves her."

"Since the class ends this week, I told her I'd find someone to cover the last class."

Owen nodded. "All right. Did she say where she was going?"

"She just said she needed to see her father." Maureen fiddled with the collar on her coat. "I hope he's okay."

"We weren't—" Owen caught himself. "I mean, she wasn't supposed to go to Wyoming for a couple more weeks." She probably would've gone sooner, but Owen had to work until December twenty-third. He normally worked holidays too, but Dr. Richards had been extremely understanding this year, and he had other faculty members who didn't have the family commitments Owen did.

"She sounded upset on the phone." Maureen glanced around, and Owen realized he'd asked the wrong person about Natalie. "I do hope her father's okay. Has she said anything to you?"

"She must be in the mountain pass," he said. "My calls go right to voicemail." Not entirely true, but seeing as every call had eventually gone to voicemail, he didn't feel too badly about the little fib. "I'm sure she's fine. I'll let you know when I hear from her." He moved away quickly, checked out, and hurried back to her house.

With the furnace fixed and pumping warmth into her house, he called her again, praying with everything he had that she'd answer this time.

"Owen," she said, and relief cascaded through him so strongly he collapsed onto her couch.

"Natalie," he breathed.

She exhaled. "I wish you wouldn't say my name like that."

"Where are you, sweetheart?"

"I wish you wouldn't call me sweetheart."

Life zoomed out, and Owen felt so far from her. From all of civilization. He needed help to get back where he belonged, and he poured out the desires of his heart to the Lord. Just like he had when dealing with Davy, he pleaded that the words he needed would drop into his mouth.

"Remember when Pastor Palmer said we needed to find something good to focus on in our lives?" he asked.

"Yeah." She sounded dubious, and he didn't blame her. He wasn't quite sure where he was going with this thought.

"I wasn't sure what that meant for me. My entire life had been turned upside down when my sister and her husband died and I got Marie. I already felt lost, and like I didn't have anything else to give, and there he was, asking us to pursue something more."

He paused for a moment, trying to organize his

thoughts. "I thought I should focus on you," he said quietly, his voice almost silent. "And it felt too easy, because you were already in my life, so willing to forgive and so easy to fall in love with."

"Is that supposed to make me feel better?" The arctic bite in her voice wasn't hard to hear.

"I don't know," he admitted. "But I thought the Lord might want me to do something a little harder. So I chose my boys. I really wanted them to feel like someone could love them, despite the bad things they'd done. I wanted them to know I loved them, and that God loved them."

"I'm sure they feel that way, Owen."

"You're probably right," he said. "The problem was, in doing that, I neglected you and Marie." His internal organs seemed so tangled, so twisted. "I didn't mean to do that. You have to believe I didn't mean to do that."

"I don't know what to believe anymore. I just know I'm really tired."

"Of me?"

"No, maybe, yes. "

That single word—*yes*—knifed through him, left him gasping for air.

"I'm sorry," she said. "I feel...I feel like no matter what I do, no matter how often I have dinner on the table and anticipate your every need, that it will never be enough. That *I* will never be enough." She exhaled and continued before Owen could assure her that she already was enough, simply by being her. "I just need a few days to figure things out."

"Where are you?"

"Almost to Butte."

"Are you on your way to Wyoming?"

"I was, but now I'm not sure. I haven't called my mom or anything." She inhaled, and he imagined her hazel eyes as they would be staring at him, searching his face. "Honestly, I just want to come home."

"I fixed your furnace," he said.

"You did what?"

"I came over to find you and apologize, hopefully take you to breakfast, but you weren't here. I noticed it was frigid in here, and I fixed the furnace."

"So you broke into my house." The playful, familiar tease made his heart flinch and a smile to flicker on his face.

"Yes, sweetheart. I broke into your house. I was—I *am*— desperate to see you. I didn't realize how much I'd hurt you when I left years ago. I mean, I thought I knew, but I didn't. I didn't know until I entered your house and realized you were gone. That you'd left, that I might never see you again, or talk to you again, or—" His voice choked and he pressed his eyes closed until he regained his composure. "I will never be able to fix that mistake. I've been wondering for the past few hours if it's something I'll have to live with for the rest of my life. It seems unfair that something I did as a dumb teenager will haunt me forever."

As Owen spoke, he realized why he connected so strongly with his boys. He coached them to move past their young, stupid mistakes. Encouraged them that they could still lead good lives, find happiness, if they started making the right decisions.

But he knew that sometimes decisions impacted a life forever. And not just one life, but many lives.

"Some decisions are life-changing," she said.

"Some are," he agreed. "I will apologize every day of my life. I will do everything I can to show you and tell you that I love you, that you're the most important person in my life."

"Owen," she said reprovingly. "I don't need you to do that."

"What do you need me to do?"

Several long seconds passed before she asked, "Why did you react so badly to me sending in that track?"

Owen took a few moments to examine his feelings, though he'd had plenty of time to self-reflect. "Honestly?"

"Aren't we always honest with each other, Owen?"

He chuckled, breathed, and started speaking.

———

"That song is deeply personal to me," he said. "I'm not sure what Davy told you about it, or how it came to be, but I wrote that…I wrote that song about you."

She'd known that, but she simply said, "Okay," so he'd keep talking. She'd pulled over to the shoulder of I-90, and on this winter weekend, there weren't many cars speeding past.

"And I wasn't ready to share it with you. With anyone, but especially you. I would've preferred to do that in my own way, create a memory for the two of us to share forever, get your opinion on what I should do with the song. If I should send it in, or just record it for us to dance to on our anniversary."

Natalie hadn't cried yet that day, but she did now. Owen wasn't perfect, but he was kind, and he did have a good heart.

"So that was taken from me, because I assume you listened to the song before you sent it to Universal?"

"Yes," she whispered. "And it was beautiful."

He sighed. "Thank you. I—I sang it for my boys because it seemed to heal them. It brought us together when we'd been fractured. My singing and playing meant something to them, and well, it hasn't meant much to anyone for a long time. That made me feel good."

"Your music has always meant something to me," she said.

"I know that, Nat, honestly. You always asked me about it, even when you probably didn't want to."

She had, but she bit back the confirmation. "So what are you going to do now? With the song, I mean."

"They want me to come to Nashville in January."

"And?"

"I didn't commit. I wanted to talk to you about it."

Confusion pricked her mind. "But—"

"But then I found out how they'd gotten the song, and I just sort of lost my temper."

"I didn't know you could actually do that."

"It's something I've worked on my entire life."

Natalie stared out the windshield, battling with herself. She didn't know what to do next. She had a half a tank of gas and a thousand dollars in her bank account. She wanted to go home. She wanted to make everything right with Owen.

"I need to go," she said.

"When will I see you?"

She didn't know and didn't want to promise him something she couldn't deliver. "When you see me."

"I love you."

"I'll talk to you soon." She hung up before she could repeat the sentiment to him, flip her car around, and drive the four hours back to his warm embrace. Alone in her car on the side of the freeway, she whispered, "I love you too, Owen Carr," because she did. But she felt like she needed some time to figure out how to be Natalie while with Owen.

She'd been feeding her faith since Pastor Palmer had given that sermon, so she believed she would make the right decisions, believed that the Lord would lead her down the right path if she asked.

So she closed her eyes and prayed. As she did, she set aside her own desires and demands. "I just want to know and be able to do what Thou would have me know and do."

As the wind howled past her window, she waited.

As the sun continued its journey toward its pinnacle, she waited.

As cars and trucks buzzed along the freeway, she waited.

She didn't get an answer—but she believed she would. For now, she put the car in gear, checked her mirrors and eased back onto the freeway. A half an hour later, she pulled into Butte, making a decision to treat herself to lunch and then get some Christmas shopping done.

She started at Muddy Creek, a little pub that served the best macaroni and cheese she'd ever eaten. Situations like this certainly called for high-carb foods, and she asked her waitress if there was a bakery nearby.

"Just down the street," she said. "Bread Underground. Best bread in the state."

Natalie thanked her, seriously doubting that Ginny, the bakery owner in Gold Valley, would agree with the waitress's assessment of Bread Underground.

Stuffed with pasta and cheese, Natalie wandered down the street to a local boutique. She shopped for herself, tried on a few things, looked at the touristy mugs and glass cutting boards. She bought Marie a cute pair of pajamas with a grizzly bear on them, and a Christmas ornament that said "Butte" in glittery, white writing.

A pang of homesickness hit her as she remembered Owen was going to go get a Christmas tree with Marie that weekend. He'd asked her to come help decorate it and then stay to watch Sterling Maughan as he tried to win the first X-Games of the season. Since Sterling had married a counselor at Silver Creek and made his home permanent in Gold Valley, the whole town had been rooting for his heroic comeback. It hadn't quite happened yet, but several stores around town advertised that they would be showing the games during their business hours.

"There you go." The clerk handed Natalie her bag of

goodies, snapping Nat from the day's events she'd left behind. Surely Owen hadn't gone up Bear Mountain to get a Christmas tree like he'd planned. He said he'd fixed her furnace, something Natalie felt a bit guilty about, especially if it meant Marie had to wait another week for a tree. She'd told Owen she was the only kid in her second grade class who didn't have one up yet, and he'd promised they'd get one this weekend.

She's not your daughter, Natalie told herself, but it didn't lessen the love she felt for Marie, nor her desire to shield the girl from disappointment as much as possible. After all, she'd already lost both of her parents in a terrible accident.

When Nat went back outside, she saw a hotel right next door. She paused, wondering what she should do. She wanted to get home and listen to what Pastor Palmer had to say. He only had three Sundays left before he retired, and she would miss his powerful spirit and quiet energy. If she stayed the night in Butte, she'd have to leave by six-thirty in the morning to get home, get changed, and get to church by eleven o'clock.

But it was already one-thirty, and the thought of driving another four hours today had every cell in her body rebelling. Making her decision, she moved toward the hotel to inquire about a room. They had one, and she booked it.

Across the street sat Wein's Men's Store, and she thought she might check it out and see if she could find something reasonable for Owen. One step through the door, though, and she knew everything in the store would cost a pretty penny. Still, she browsed the aisles anyway, bypassing the sportcoats and suits. She'd never seen Owen wear much more than jeans and a white shirt to church, but she thought a tie might be a good idea.

As she fingered the silk neckties, a salesman approached. "Can I help you find something?"

"Do you sell cowboy hats?" she asked.

He smiled. "We don't. We only have caps. If you're looking for a cowboy hat, I'd try Ward's."

"Hmm." She nodded. "What about cowboy boots? Do you do special orders?"

The salesman helped her order a pair of custom-sized boots for Owen, and she left the store knowing the boots would show up at her sister's house in Peach Valley. She hoped she'd be there with Owen in a couple of weeks.

She wandered down the street in this obvious historic district. She thought Butte would be a great place to spend a weekend as she passed several art galleries and antique shops. But in mid-December, with the tail of a storm still hovering overhead, she just wanted to get out of the cold.

She spied a church, and ducked down the sidewalk and inside. Someone was playing the organ, and she slipped into the back row of the chapel to listen, to think, to seek more answers.

CHAPTER 20

*T*he next time Natalie slid onto a bench in a chapel, it was the next morning and the congregation in Gold Valley was already standing, singing the opening hymn. She hadn't told Owen she'd be at church that day. She had texted him to say she was staying in Butte last night. To his credit, he hadn't asked when she'd come back to town. He'd simply thanked her for letting him know she was safe. He was certainly acting better than she had when he'd left town.

That's because he knows you're coming back, she thought, a shot of acid going into her stomach. At that moment, she knew.

You haven't forgiven him for leaving you behind all those years ago.

A warm feeling flowed over her like someone had turned on a soft rain of scented, heated water. At the same time, her breaths felt cold as they entered her lungs. She'd had twelve years to forgive him. She loved him. What more did she need to do that she hadn't done?

"This Christmas season, I'd like to challenge you to focus on something." Pastor Palmer stood at the pulpit now, his usual smile on his face. "The Savior could see people for who and what they truly were. I think that might be a challenge for us in the world we live in. We're bombarded by images and statuses portraying who we should be, and what we should be doing."

Natalie nodded, along with everyone in the row in front of her. Someone on the other side of the aisle from her whispered, "Mm hmm."

"I think we should strive to be more like the Savior. Look at people as who they really are: a child of God. I think if we can manage to do that, we'll forgive more easily, settle old disputes, and be kinder with each other. Most of us are ill, my friends, and I don't mean with a cold or cancer. I mean we're spiritually ill, and we could all use a smile, a hug, and an understanding heart. The Savior had a unique ability to see this in every person he met. Can we do the same?" The pastor's gaze swept the crowd. "And my dear friends, one more thing. It would be well with us if we could see others as the Lord does. But do we see ourselves that way too? Do you believe you're a child of God, that He loves you unconditionally, that you are worth His sacrifice?"

Natalie wept at the power in the pastor's words. She wanted to see people—and herself—the way the Lord did. She wanted to forgive more easily. Wanted to heal old hurts within herself and wanted to support and help others as they healed.

But she had a couple of problems. Number one, she didn't know how to view people through the Savior's eyes. And number two, she still feared that even if she could figure out how to forgive Owen, she still wouldn't be enough for him.

———

Owen fidgeted through most of church, listening and feeling the truth of Pastor Palmer's words but restless nonetheless.

He needed to see Natalie. Look into her eyes and see the woman she was. Search her soul to see if she could stay with him while he explored his options in Nashville. That much had also become clear to him in her brief absence.

He wanted to write country music. He needed to. Something about composing the music and searching for the exact right lyrics bled the negative emotion from him. And he needed that outlet to be mentally healthy.

"And now, you all get to try exactly what I've asked you to do." He gestured to someone sitting on the front row. "I've asked my successor to speak with us today, and next week he will give the entire sermon. Doctor Pinnion." Pastor Palmer backed up as the tall, dark-skinned man mounted the steps and took his place in front of the microphone.

Pastor Palmer grinned and bent to adjust the mic to a

higher position. Dr. Pinnion stared out at the crowd, his dark, deep eyes drinking them in. Owen felt the man's spirit, and it was strong.

"My brothers and sisters," he said. When he spoke, the air vibrated because of the bass quality of his voice. "It is good to be here with you today. Your spirits are strong, and I am grateful God has led me to Gold Valley."

Owen wanted to add an "Amen," to that statement, because he also felt called to Gold Valley—which made his desire to work in country music that much more confusing. He needed to riddle it all out, make all the pieces line up.

He glanced over his shoulder, like the woman he sought would suddenly appear. He needed to talk to Natalie.

At the same time, his mind rebelled from the idea because his heart wouldn't stop screaming a warning. At some point, he'd have to put her first, and he knew she wouldn't stick around forever, waiting for him to do that. In fact, she might decide a relationship with him was too complex if he sought her opinion about Nashville, if he asked her to care for Marie full-time so he could go to Nashville, if he had to leave Gold Valley in favor of Nashville.

Fear ruled him, and he wondered how he could prioritize Natalie when he also had Marie, his music, and his boys to consider. A voice inside whispered that he couldn't do it all, but he couldn't see himself giving up any of them. Not again.

And so he found himself between those reins again, not really sure if he should pull right or left, gripping them too tight so the horse couldn't take a step at all. That was how he felt: Trapped, with multiple ways out as long as someone else paid the sacrifice for him.

Without word from Natalie, Owen loaded Marie in his truck and went over to his parent's house for dinner. He had plenty of money to eat out, but he liked a home-cooked meal better than anything he could get in a restaurant. Like a punch to the gut, he realized he'd taken Natalie's culinary skills for granted.

"You go on in," he told Marie as he pulled into the driveway. "Tell Grandma I'll be in in a sec." He got out his phone and sent a text to Natalie.

Missing you today. He glanced up and out the windshield, wondering how he could convey his longing for her in only a few words. That was the part of songwriting that the music took care of. The way he sang the lyrics gave them a different emotion, made them come alive, made them more than words. The chords he matched the words with brought even more meaning, deeper understanding.

He couldn't appropriately tell her how he was feeling in a text. So he sent just those three words and trudged up the shoveled sidewalk to his parents' front door. He entered the house to the sound of laughter, and it made him pause. His parents had been struggling to come to terms with Tasha's death, and Owen had no idea how to help them.

But there was his mother, her head tipped back as she

laughed at something Marie had said. The girl giggled and said, "Help me with my apron, Grandma."

His mother gazed at her tenderly as she lifted Marie's hair and tied the apron around her neck. "There you go, princess. Now." She turned. "For oven pancakes, we need a dozen eggs. Do you think you can crack that many?"

Marie's eyes looked like someone had lit a fire behind them. "Yes!"

"Right there in that bowl." His mother turned and caught sight of Owen. He lifted his hand in a greeting of hello, and she said, "Owen," warmly before turning back to what smelled like bacon on the stove.

He moved into the kitchen and gave his mother a kiss on the cheek and a squeeze. "Hey, Ma."

"Where's Natalie today?" she asked, still poking at the sizzling bacon with a pair of tongs.

"She—" Owen started, but Marie said, "She left town," Marie said. "Her furnace was broken, and she was cold. But she left us a lot of chili." She cracked another egg against the counter and swooped it up to the bowl before any of the white could leak.

"Is that right?" his mom asked.

"Yup," Marie said. "She'll be back soon." She looked at Owen, her eyes wide and round and beautiful. "Right, Uncle Owen? Natalie will be back soon."

"Right," he said, but his voice fell short of reassuring. He hadn't heard from her since last night, and he wasn't sure what she would consider pushy. "Where's Dad?" he asked his mother.

"Out feeding the chickens and rabbits."

"Oh, no," Marie said, and Owen's gaze flew to hers, expecting a yolky mess.

He saw nothing. "What is it, baby doll?"

"I like to go out with him to feed the chickens and rabbits."

"He went out just before you got here," Owen's mother said. "Get your coat on and go find him. I think Owen can take over cracking the eggs."

Marie jumped off the stool, flung her arms into her jacket, and raced out the backdoor. Owen took her place in front of the egg carton. "You might be wrong about me and these eggs," he said, his large hands barely able to hold the egg. He managed to clink it against the side of the bowl until it broke enough or him to break the shell apart.

"So, Natalie left town? Or she just went out of town?"

So his mother had picked up on the slightly odd wording. "She...did both," Owen said. "She's staying in Butte for a few days."

"Are you still going to Wyoming with her for Christmas?"

Owen sighed and almost smashed his eggshell into smithereens. "I don't know, Ma."

She stepped away from the stove and moved next to him. "What do you mean you don't know?"

He stared down at her, but she didn't flinch away from his gaze the way some people did. "I mean I lost my temper with her, and things...sort of blew up."

"That's why she left town."

LIZ ISAACSON

Owen nodded and selected another egg from the carton. "I talked to her on the phone yesterday. She texted that she was staying in Butte last night."

"Did you call her today?"

"Do you think I should?"

"Owen," his mother said in a placating tone. "Do you love this woman?"

"Yeah, Ma." Owen sighed again, this time the sound full of longing instead of fueled by frustration. "Yeah, I love her."

"Does she know you love her?"

"I've told her a couple of times."

Several beats of silence passed while Owen wrestled with the egg and his mom watched him. She finally said, "Hmm," and moved back to the stove.

"So should I call her?"

"She probably would've liked a call this morning," his mother said. "To find out if she was going to be at church so you could save her a seat."

"I—" Owen clamped his mouth closed and cracked another egg, his mind set on warp speed. "I was giving her some distance," he said. "She said she needed time to figure things out."

"Sure, but time doesn't mean silence." She reached past him and extracted a plate from the cupboard. "Bacon's done." She rested her elbow on the counter. "You know, if I'd been told one thing, but then a person's actions said something else, I'd be pretty confused."

Owen barely refrained from rolling his eyes. "All right, Ma. I'll call her."

THE COWBOY AND THE NANNY

"Good." She smiled at him as she tonged bacon from the pan to the plate. "Now tell me what you lost your temper over."

"A song." He finished with the eggs and rinsed his hands.

His mom had abandoned the bacon completely. She stared at him. "You're writing songs again?"

He couldn't tell if she was more shocked, more horrified, or more excited. He took the tongs from her and finished the job of removing the bacon from the pan. "Yes, Mother. I like writing songs. It makes me...feel something good. It—it takes all these negative things I feel, all this sadness and longing and depression, and it bleeds onto the page, into the song. Then it's not inside me anymore."

"I've seen you happier these past several months," she said, her voice barely audible. "I thought it was because of Natalie."

"It was. The song is about her. She...." He didn't quite know how to put into words what Natalie was to him, how he'd felt her influence in his life, over his heart, guiding his decisions, since the day he'd met her. "She's inspired a lot of my songs," he said. "Nearly all of them on my first album are about her, or what I wished had happened with her, or from something I learned or did when I was with her." He shrugged. "This time, I expect it'll be about the same."

His mom wiped her eyes. "You two are somethin' special."

He grunted, because he wasn't entirely sure they were still together. "I wrote the song and played it for my boys at Silver Creek. They wanted to record it, so I did. One of them gave the track to Nat, and she sent it to the VP at Universal Music Group."

"And that's why you got mad." She wasn't asking, and she turned away to collect her recipe book. She added salt and flour to the eggs, a splash of milk and a bowlful of melted butter. Owen watched her bring together the oven pancake batter, his mind far away.

"Why are you still standin' there?" His mother made a ruckus as she got out a sheet pan. "Go call that woman and invite her over for oven pancakes and bacon."

Owen snapped to attention and walked into the living room to make the call, hoping for some measure of privacy, but the way his mother hovered near the mouth of the kitchen, he didn't think he'd get it.

CHAPTER 21

"*H*ey," he breathed into the phone when Natalie answered. "So I'm at my parents', and this might be a long shot, but I'm wondering if you're anywhere nearby and can possibly come over for the best oven pancakes you'll ever eat." He pressed his eyes closed and waited.

She laughed, which Owen took as a good sign. Relief spread through him with the speed of lightning, and it felt just as electric and hot.

"I happen to be just sitting down to eat with my friends," she said. "But maybe I can sneak away in a few minutes."

His heart felt like it had been attached to a yo-yo. It went up and down, up and down. "So you'll come?"

"Hmm...can I wear my stretchy pants?"

He couldn't help it—he burst into laughter. "I can't wait to see them." He hung up and spun back to his mother. "She's coming."

She smiled and glanced toward the window overlooking the backyard. "I knew she would."

Owen wished he had his mother's confidence, but his nerves assaulted him, especially because she hadn't said she'd rush right over, hadn't been willing to completely abandon her friends for him.

At the same time, he reasoned that she had done exactly that for the past several months. He knew she used to spend Sundays with them, but she'd been devoting her time to him and Marie since August.

He coached himself not to be impatient, but he couldn't help keeping one eye on the clock as the pancakes came out of the oven, as his mother heated the syrup and called everyone to the dining room table. One extra plate sat on the counter, and Owen glared at it like it was the reason Natalie hadn't come yet. But deep down in his soul, he knew *he* was the reason for her absence.

———

Natalie nibbled on vegetables as Stephanie talked about the dance studio manager. They hadn't been getting along, which was nothing new. Natalie had heard it all before, experienced a lot of Stephanie's complaints herself. She was sympathetic and gave Stephanie a hug. "I'm sorry, sweetie."

"It's not like I'm going to quit or anything."

"Of course not." Natalie had never considered leaving the studio, though there were things about it she didn't like.

Jason broke into their conversation with, "Did you guys see Sterling win last night?"

Stephanie's face brightened, and she placed a pasta salad on the table as she said, "Wasn't he amazing? Did you guys see Norah cheering in the crowd?" She sighed like it was her romance being played out on television. "They are so cute together."

Natalie hadn't seen it, so she let the conversation flow over and around her, nodding and smiling in appropriate places. She picked at her food, wondering what an oven pancake was and if she should save a lot of room for them.

Don't be ridiculous, she told herself. *They're probably done eating by now.* A glance at the clock confirmed that it was almost five o'clock, and the Carr's ate at four.

Stephanie caught her looking at the clock. "Is everything okay?" Her eyes darted to her phone. "Hey, who called earlier?"

"Owen." Natalie flipped her phone over, and over, drawing the attention of Jason and Bea. She hadn't told anyone that she'd left town for a day, that she was having doubts about Owen, about everything.

Stephanie cocked her head. "I thought it was weird you came tonight."

"I've been coming." Natalie reached for her water glass.

"Not since you started dating the hottest bachelor in town." Bea glanced at Jason, who rolled his eyes.

"There are a lot of bachelors in town," he said.

"He's just the best looking," Bea insisted. "So why are you here instead of with him?"

Natalie lifted one shoulder in a very unconvincing shrug. "It's complicated."

Stephanie scoffed. "I don't believe that."

"Owen is more complicated than you might think," she said. "And there are a lot of issues from the past."

Stephanie collected her plate and took it into the kitchen. "You gotta leave the past in the past, Nat."

"He invited me to dinner at his parents." She took her dishes to the sink too.

"Just now? Tonight?"

"Yeah."

"Why are you still here?" Stephanie stared at her like she'd grown an extra head.

"I wasn't just going to run out on you guys." She looked at Stephanie and Jason and Bea. "You guys are like *my* family."

"Maybe you should bring Owen here next week," Jason said. "He should get to meet your family."

"We were supposed to go to Wyoming for him to meet my parents. I mean, he's met them before, obviously. But…." She trailed off, not quite sure how to finish the sentence.

"If I remember right." Bea added her dirty dishes to the pile with a loud clattering sound. "Owen wasn't particularly loquacious."

"English, Bea," Jason said.

"He didn't have a lot to say."

"What does that have to do with anything?"

"It means that maybe Natalie should listen to what he *does* say. Take it at face value."

Jason chuckled. "Not everyone is like you, Bea."

"And what does that mean?" She cocked her hip and glared at him.

"It means that if you took your own advice, maybe you and me—" He cut off and glared at her for a moment longer, a redness entering his face. Natalie watched them both like they were the most fascinating tennis match she'd ever seen, her gaze volleying back and forth between them until Jason shook his head and walked toward the front door. He calmly collected his coat from the rack, put it on, and said, "Thank you for dinner, Steph. It was delicious, as always."

He slipped into the night, the door behind him echoing with finality. Bea deflated then, and Stephanie slid her arm around her shoulders. "I didn't know you and Jason had a thing."

"We don't."

"What was that about then?"

Bea glanced at Natalie. "It's complicated."

A small smile stole across Natalie's face. "I get complicated."

"You should go see Owen," Bea said, to which Stephanie vehemently nodded.

Natalie's stomach clenched, but she said, "Yeah, I guess I should." She hugged her girlfriends and grabbed her keys from the counter. "Thanks for dinner, Steph." She turned back. "Maybe I will bring Owen next Sunday."

"He's welcome to come." Stephanie grinned. "No text needed."

"He can eat a lot."

Stephanie gestured to the copious leftovers. "I think I can handle him."

Natalie giggled and left the house, her nerves turning to ice as she entered the frosty night. The drive to Owen's parents' house took twenty minutes, by which time she was sure Owen would've left. He didn't normally stay long after dinner ended. At least he hadn't when she was with him. Maybe he did otherwise.

His truck sat in the driveway, causing her heart to tap, tap, tap against her ribs. Part of her wanted to meet him privately, and the other part was relieved that there would be witnesses. She parked behind him and knocked on the front door, her fingers refusing to release from the fist afterward. She shoved her hands in her pockets and waited.

The door opened only a few moments later, and Owen stood there in all his cowboy glory. The gray hat he'd taken to wearing made his eyes seem more coal-colored than blue, and they watched her with an intensity she hadn't experienced before.

"Natalie." He said the three syllables of her name with reverence.

"Can I come in? It's freezing out here."

He stepped back to reveal an empty living room, and her anxiety amped up again. "Where is everyone?"

"Marie convinced them to watch the Smurfs." Owen grinned and shook his head. "They're downstairs." He nodded toward the kitchen. "You want some coffee?"

She smiled. "Coffee would be great. Sorry I missed dinner."

He went in front of her and busied himself making coffee. "Oven pancakes really are spectacular," he said. "I'll get the recipe from my mom and you can make them whenever you want." With everything set and the coffee maker bubbling, he turned toward her. "I'm so glad you came." His hand flinched toward hers before he glued it to his side.

She stepped into his personal space and reached for his cowboy hat. She tugged it off his head, expecting him to protest, but he simply let her, their eyes locked as the tether that had cemented between them at that swim meet bound them together again.

"Did you figure things out?" he asked, his voice made mostly of air.

She shook her head, trying to see him the way she needed to. She didn't want to feel abandoned every time something in his life took him from her. It was unreasonable that they would be together twenty-four hours a day. She didn't want to remember how she'd felt when he'd left every time they disagreed.

She wanted to forgive him.

Please help me forgive him, she prayed as she gazed at him. *I love him. Help me move past what's happened between us.*

She wasn't sure what she was expecting, but it wasn't for a feeling of peace to flood her, making her gasp though it was a pleasing sensation.

"Nat? You okay?"

She curled one hand along the back of his neck, her fingertips brushing the ends of his hair. "I love you," she whispered. "I think I've figured at least that much out."

He grinned, his arms finally encircling her and gifting her with that beautiful sense of protection. "I love you too, Natalie." He dipped his mouth to hers, and she kissed him slowly, feeling something new in this kiss she hadn't in any of the previous kisses they'd shared.

She felt whole now, like she was a new person. A new person who could finally start to look forward instead of gripping tightly to something she'd been dragging behind her all this time.

She kissed him until her lips felt swollen and the kitchen had grown as hot as the boiling coffee. Then she leaned her cheek against his pulse, which *ba-bumped* rapidly.

"I will do better," he whispered.

"What will you do better?" she asked. "Because that kiss was pretty dang perfect."

He chuckled and squeezed her tighter. "I will do better at putting you first." He stepped back, cleared his throat, and reached for a coffee mug. "But I do want to talk about Nashville."

The heat inside her cooled and she accepted the coffee mug from him and sipped it in an attempt to feel warm again. But it didn't work. Something as simple as a hot drink could never replace the warmth that came from Owen's love.

"What about it?" she asked.

"Don't freak out," he warned, positioning himself against the sink, several paces from her. "I think we should move there."

She choked on her coffee, going from calm to freak-out

mode in a single breath. "Move there?" Her mind raced around her dance classes, the cooking classes, her library board service, his boys, and Marie.

"You hate winter," he said. "It's milder there. I need to go meet with the execs in January, but I won't go without you."

She hated that her next thought was about the cost of traveling to Nashville, of moving there. It wasn't like she and Owen were married—not even close. Even if he asked her in the next moment to marry him, such an event was months off. He hadn't even met her parents yet.

"Owen—what about Marie? She's in school here, and she has friends, and your parents, and.... We can't move to Nashville. Henry's parents are in Idaho. When will she ever see them?"

Owen's eyes darkened, and he exhaled in frustration. "I don't know. Nothing is lining up in my head."

"You want to make another album."

"Yes."

"And you can't do it here."

"I probably could, but all the contractual stuff has to be worked out first. That could take a couple of months."

Natalie frowned, her mind operating on overdrive. "Leave Marie here with me. I can keep teaching my classes, and I'll take care of her. You go take care of what you need to, and then come back."

He shook his head, his mouth flattening into a straight line. "I will not leave you here, not again."

"What about your job?" What she really wanted to ask

was: *What about my job?* Sure, Owen might not need a job in order to live and pay bills, but Natalie sure did.

He sighed and looked out the window over the sink. "I love my job at Silver Creek, love those boys, love the horses. But Silver Creek will be there in a year, or two years, or five years. I feel like…I feel like if I don't do this now, I'll lose my opportunity."

Natalie took a step toward him, and he swung his attention to her. "So you're panicking again."

"No." His shoulders dropped. "Maybe a little."

"Do you feel like you need to decide today?"

"Not necessarily."

Natalie pasted a smile on her face. "All right then. Let's be thinking about solutions and stuff, but you don't need to decide today."

"It's not just about me."

"Of course. Have you talked to Marie about it?"

He shook his head. "It's something I've been thinking about since the sermon this morning."

"That was a powerful challenge, wasn't it?"

"I've been so focused on trying to fix everything I did twelve years ago, but I realized that I haven't actually forgiven myself. But just now—" He waved to where he used to be standing. "Just now, I felt this powerful impression that I've set right what I did wrong, and that I should forgive myself."

She nodded, knowing exactly how he felt. "And now you're ready to move forward."

"Right. With you, though, Natalie. I want us to make decisions together."

Natalie cocked her head to the side and a coy smile played with her lips. "Sounds like something a husband and wife would do."

He blinked at her. "Are you saying we need to be married to make decisions like this?"

She hadn't come intending to pressure him about marrying her. The idea hadn't even been near her mind. "That sounds about right." She walked over to him and took his hands in hers. "Owen Carr, will you marry me?"

CHAPTER 22

"*I* like that one." Marie pointed to a square diamond the size of Natalie's knuckle.

"That one's too big," she said. "Your uncle—"

"Has plenty of money," Owen breathed into her ear. "If you like it, try it on."

Natalie glanced up at him though he stood so close behind her, she had to really crane her neck to see his face. "We'll need that money to move across the country."

"I asked you to pick out the one you like."

"I like several of them." She glanced back in the jewelry case and pointed to the square diamond ring Marie had indicated. "I guess let me see that one."

The jeweler pulled it out and handled it with care as he slid it onto Natalie's ring finger. She gazed at the stone, pure happiness radiating through her.

"I like that one," Marie repeated, her eyes shining with delight.

Natalie smiled at her. "It is a nice one."

"So, is that the one?" Owen glanced at his phone in an obvious show of checking the time.

"Are you in a hurry?"

"Kind of, yeah," he said. "We're leaving for Wyoming in the morning, and I still haven't packed."

Natalie tipped her head back and laughed. "You've had the last three days off, and you haven't managed to do your laundry, is that it?"

"I used to have someone doing that for me," he said dryly. "And we still have to go to dinner too." He leaned closer and dropped his voice as he said, "And I may have some presents I need to wrap so Santa can find Marie in Peach Valley."

Natalie gazed up at him, joy dancing through her system. Joy that he and Marie were coming to Wyoming with her for Christmas. Joy that she'd be wearing his engagement ring when they arrived in Wyoming for Christmas. Joy that he'd said yes when she'd asked him to marry her and then go to Wyoming for Christmas.

"All right," she said, imitating his cowboy drawl. "This is the one." She slid it off and handed it back to the jeweler. "And it even fits."

"Let me get it cleaned for you," he said. "While I do that, Perry will take care of the payment."

Natalie wandered away from the counter while Owen pulled out his credit card. She didn't want to know the final price, and she bent her head close to Marie as the girl looked at a row of pink-stoned rings.

"Hey, sweetheart," she said. "How are you doing with this? You know, me and your uncle getting married?"

Owen said he'd talked to Marie about it, and she'd been happy with the idea of Natalie living with them all the time and being Owen's wife.

Marie shrugged. "You're a good cook, and Grandma says you make Uncle Owen really happy."

"What about you?" Natalie asked. "Are you happy?"

Marie fixed her dark blue eyes on Natalie's. "I like you, Nat. You're nice." A timid smile came across her face and her chin wobbled. "I miss my mom and dad."

Natalie wrapped Marie into a solid hug. "I know you do, baby doll. I am not replacing your mom. I love you, though, and I'll help you remember your mom and dad."

Marie nodded into Natalie's shoulder, where her warm tears stained Natalie's sweater. When she quieted, Natalie pulled back. "I knew your mom, you know. She was a cheerleader in high school. Did you know that?"

Marie sniffed and wiped her eyes. "Grandma showed me some pictures and her uniform."

"She was always nice to me," Natalie said. "When your uncle and I were dating in high school, your mom always made me feel welcome at your grandma's house. I appreciated that about her."

Marie watched her with wide eyes. "What else do you know about her?"

Natalie smiled and tucked her hand in Marie's. "Well, let's see...."

Owen twisted toward Natalie, feeling huge and out of place behind the wheel of her sedan. He'd wanted to drive his truck, but there was literally nowhere to put the presents and luggage for three people without it getting wet on the drive down. And her car had handled the roads just fine.

"Are you sure they're not going to be waiting with tar and pitchforks?" he asked. "Do I turn here?"

"Up there." She pointed to the next street, where the light was red. "And I told them I was bringing you with me, and to be nice."

"That doesn't mean they won't have pitchforks," he muttered as he coasted to a stop behind another car waiting to turn right.

"I doubt my father even knows what a pitchfork is," Natalie said.

"He lived in Montana for thirty years," Owen said. "Of course he knows what a pitchfork is." His stomach wouldn't settle down, and his tone came out a bit frostier than he'd intended. "Sorry," he said. "I don't know why I'm so nervous." But he did. Natalie had told him how her parents had reacted to his sudden departure twelve years ago. Again, he felt like that single decision had spurred a lifetime of pain, that he'd be punished forever because of one thing he'd done twelve years ago.

Of course, he knew it was more than one thing. He hadn't called the way he should have. He hadn't come back the way he'd promised. He hadn't done a lot of things he should've. But he didn't let it bother him anymore—he'd found his forgiveness. Natalie had forgiven him, and that was all that mattered.

After all, he didn't have to live with her mom or her dad. Just had to make it through holidays.

He took a deep breath as she pointed to a sprawling, brown-brick house. "That's it," she said. "Remember Julie? She's a little...intense."

"Your sister was crazy," he said.

"Hey." Natalie glanced to the backseat where Marie sat. "Sisters are wonderful." She winked at Marie. "Mine does happen to be a little crazy. I like to think of her as eccentric."

"What does that mean?" Marie asked.

"Crazy," Owen said with a smile. He peered at the house, his emotions spiraling up and then down. He could employ his politeness, no matter what anyone said or did. Only Natalie's and Marie's opinions mattered to him anyhow. "All right," he drawled. "Let's go meet the family."

Natalie knocked and entered first, tugging Marie by the hand behind her. Owen waited until they'd both entered, until he heard Julie's delighted squeals, before he went inside and pushed the door closed behind him.

Julie was crouched down in front of Marie, stroking her hair and exclaiming over its beauty. She took the girl's coat, and then hugged Natalie so tight and so long that Owen wondered if Nat would pass out from lack of air. When Julie trained her gaze on him, Owen tipped his hat to her. "Hey, Julie. Nice to see you again."

"Oh, you." She swatted his bicep and reached for his

jacket, which he gave her gladly. "At least you didn't call me ma'am. But I would use ma'am when you meet Mom. Word to the wise."

"Noted," Owen said, glancing over Julie's shoulder with rioting nerves contained neatly beneath his skin. "Where are your parents?"

"Kitchen. Go, go." Julie shooed Natalie and Marie through the doorway, but she went down the hall to deposit their coats in the bedroom.

Natalie reached for Owen's hand before she entered the kitchen, and her tight squeeze indicated that she had some of her own anxiety to deal with. He hated that he'd been the cause of that, but again, there was nothing he could do about it now. They'd discussed at length how her parents would receive him, and now the moment had come.

"Mom," Natalie said. "We're here, and—"

Her mother turned from the stove, a wide smile on her face. "Oh, my goodness. Is this an angel?" She beamed at Marie with love in her eyes. "Look how big you've gotten, Miss Marie."

"Miss Brooke?" Marie glanced back at Owen. "You didn't say we'd be seein' Miss Brooke!" She launched herself into Natalie's mother's arms, who held her tight and pressed her eyes closed. She held the girl and looked right into her face. "Are you bein' good for your uncle?"

"Yes, ma'am," Marie said. "He's gettin' married soon."

"I know." Her eyes finally moved to Natalie. "He's marryin' my daughter."

Marie looked back and forth between the two women. "I

like her," she told Natalie's mom in a not-so-quiet voice. "Uncle Owen does too. He kisses her a lot."

Natalie gasped, and Owen's face flushed as he said, "All right, Marie—" at the same time Natalie's mother threw a laugh toward the ceiling.

When she quieted, she said, "I hope he does kiss her a lot, Marie. That's what you do when you're in love." She set Marie on her feet and embraced Natalie. When she stepped over to Owen, he felt nothing but love in her arms, and acceptance when she said, "It's about time you became part of our family, Owen Carr."

He stepped back, the words he wanted to say trapped behind the emotion caught in his throat. He nodded and caught Natalie swiping at her eyes.

"What did I miss?" Julie came bustling into the kitchen. "Mom, you stopped stirring the creamed corn?" She grabbed the wooden spoon and began swishing for all she was worth.

"I was meeting everyone," she said. "It's not even boiling yet."

"How do you know Marie?" Owen asked.

"She was in my Sunday children's class." Natalie's mom smiled down at Marie. "Was years ago, but I never forget the good ones."

Marie beamed up at her and then tucked one hand back into Owen's and one into Natalie's. "Where's Papa Bear?"

Natalie choked. "She doesn't mean Dad, does she?"

Her mother held her head high and said, "He was quite pleasant with the children."

Julie glanced over, a giggle escaping as she continued to babysit the creamed corn.

Natalie's mom bent down and whispered, "Papa Bear is taking a nap downstairs. Should we go wake him up?" She extended her hand for Marie to take and led her around the corner and down the steps.

Owen watched them go, his heart about to burst with relief and joy and gratitude. Natalie nudged him with her shoulder and he took her into his arms, beyond glad she was his and he was hers.

Later that night, after Natalie had worked her magic with cream, sugar, and chocolate and they all had a piece of pie and a cup of coffee, her mother asked, "So are you two going to stay in Gold Valley?"

"We're getting married there," Natalie hedged, meeting Owen's eye. His pulse picked up and he put his fork down.

"We're thinkin' about moving to Nashville," he said. "I have the opportunity to make another record."

Brooke exchanged a glance with her husband, who'd been nice and cordial to Owen, but not overly welcoming at the same time. He shook his head as if he couldn't believe history was about to repeat itself.

"They have great ballet schools there," Natalie said. "I'd keep teaching. And Marie would go to school, of course."

"When's the wedding?" Julie asked.

"May," Natalie said. "So we wouldn't go until then." She reached for Owen's hand and he gave it to her, gave her all his strength. He'd give her anything he could. "Owen will likely go in January for a few weeks. Once the contract is sorted out and signed, he'll come back to Gold Valley, we'll get married, and pack up, and then move."

"We've already asked Pastor Palmer to marry us," Owen added.

"I thought he was retiring," Natalie's mom said.

"He is," Nat said. "This Sunday is his last, but he'll still be in town, and we booked the church, and he said he would love to do it." She smiled at Owen, and he returned the gesture, glad everything she wanted for her wedding seemed to be falling into place.

———

Three Sundays later, Owen sat in the congregation with his fiancée and his daughter, trying to find something in Dr. Pinnion's sermon that didn't make him angry. But everything he said about trials and weathering them well rubbed him the wrong way.

He leaned over and said, "I have to go," to Natalie before practically sprinting from the chapel. Once outside, away from the man's deep voice, Owen pressed his back into the wall by the activity board and breathed.

He'd been working on removing that layer of waxed paper between him and God. It was very nearly transparent now, but Owen still felt the barrier there. He pushed against it, but it didn't budge, didn't break.

And he just couldn't understand why God had taken Tasha and Henry. So his parents could struggle with grief and depression for almost a year? So an eight-year-old could grow to forget her own parents? So he could prove himself worthy by taking in a daughter? How did that make him a better person than he was before? How did his mother's crying help her?

Owen shook his head, confusion and grief and fury flooding him. He'd managed to box everything up over the past twelve months when it came to Tasha and Henry. He'd worked on himself when it came to Natalie, and he had devoted himself to providing for Marie.

But he just didn't understand how a loving, merciful God could do what He'd done. Couldn't believe He'd punish a child so that the adults around her could prove their faithfulness.

Heavy footsteps came his way, and he cast his eyes heavenward, still relying on the strength of a God he believed in and loved, but simply didn't understand.

"Owen." His father's voice brought a flash flood of tears to Owen's eyes. He pushed them back when he saw his own agony reflected in his father's eyes. He didn't know what to say, so he kept quiet. His dad clearly had the same problem, and they stood together in companionable silence.

Finally Owen asked, "How's Mom?"

"She's getting better," his dad said. "The therapy has been helping a lot, actually."

"The anniversary of their deaths is next week," Owen whispered. "I don't—I don't know what to do for Marie."

"Has she been askin' about it?"

He shook his head. "But Natalie thinks we should bring it up. Says it's not healthy to let a child come to us with all the questions. Says we should be open and communicative about Tasha and Henry and how we're feeling about them and all that." Every time Owen thought about his sister, exhaustion overcame him. He couldn't think much past that, and he didn't have answers for Natalie when she asked him how he felt.

"That Natalie is a smart woman," his dad said. "Will you be here next week?"

"Yes, I'm leaving for Nashville the following day." He'd planned the trip specifically so he'd be in town, to support Marie, to support his parents. He was beginning to wonder who was supporting him.

All at once, like a gust of chilly winter air, a feeling overcame him. The hair on the back of his neck stood up and he knew.

God loved him. God had not abandoned him. God would support him through this next week, this next year, and all the years to come.

The tears returned, and this time Owen did not suck them back inside. They ran down his face as his father embraced him.

CHAPTER 23

*D*espite the fact that Owen didn't have to be at Silver Creek by six o'clock anymore, he still woke before the sun. He still got up and put on a pot of coffee before he showered. He still wore his cowboy hat and kept quiet so he wouldn't wake Marie.

He plucked chords and ran through lyrics in his head, writing things down and scratching others out. When he woke her at seven-thirty, he played through his songs for her and told her a story about one or both of her parents. He encouraged her to ask questions, but Marie didn't really seem to have any.

The day of his sister's death dawned particularly cold. He didn't get out his guitar but sat at the kitchen table with his mug, waiting for Natalie to arrive. She blew through the front door at seven-fifteen, a beautiful, mussed addition to his life.

He kissed her quick, his nerves and exhaustion near

their breaking point. Since his revelation at church the prior week, Owen had been holding onto that feeling and praying for the emotional stability and strength he needed. Problem was, he never really knew how much he needed, and he often felt like he came up short.

At the same time, he hadn't been able to bring himself to go to church just a few days ago. He didn't want to be angry again, didn't want to question himself, didn't want to break down. Natalie had come and taken Marie, and he'd told her everything he felt, everything he thought about.

"I'll go get Marie," he said, still unsure of what he wanted to tell her that day. He smiled, at peace for several breaths, as he stood in her bedroom doorway and watched her sleep. She really was angelic with her white-blonde hair fanned around her face. The love he felt increased, doubled and then tripled, and he wondered if her parents were watching over her.

Of course they are, he thought, and the idea brought him so much comfort. It also lifted the weight he felt. Marie didn't have to rely on Owen alone. She could rely on the Lord too.

He crossed to her bedside and woke her. "Will you come on out to the kitchen?" he asked. "Nat's here and we want to talk to you."

She slipped her hand into his and they walked down the hall together.

"Hiya, baby," Natalie said, pulling Marie into a gentle embrace. "Did you sleep good?"

"Yeah." Marie yawned as she bent down and patted Tar

Baby's head. Natalie collected Marie into her lap and looked at Owen.

"Marie," he said, taking his spot at the table. He looked into her eyes, and all the carefully planned things he was going to say vanished. "Your mom could peel an apple in one, long piece." He smiled as the memory washed over him like summer rain. "Once, Grandma had to leave us home alone, and I wanted an apple but I don't like the peels. So your mom got out a knife and she started peeling it for me. She showed me how to do it, but every time I tried, the knife would slip."

He grinned and a light chuckle slipped from his lips. "When Grandma got home, she sure was mad that we'd peeled every apple in the house but only eaten one."

Marie smiled and giggled with him, the sound as healing as anything Owen had experienced. He met Natalie's eye and realized he didn't have to have all the answers, didn't have to have perfect belief, didn't have to be everything to everyone.

Gratitude filled his heart for the two people in the room with him, and for his faith in the Lord, and that was enough for now.

Owen took his faith with him to Nashville, where he really needed it. He relied on his gut and the Lord's strength as he met with Jim Guthrie and everyone else at the Universal Media Group. The producer of his previous album no longer worked at the company, and Owen took a few days to meet with other producers. He paced in his hotel room and bent over the contract when it came.

He met with a real estate agent and sent pictures to Natalie of the houses he went to see. Everything felt like it was falling into place, maybe a little too fast for Owen to keep track of it all. When he felt overwhelmed, he got down on his knees, and he kept a prayer in his heart if he couldn't kneel.

After two weeks away from those he loved, he entered the offices at the Universal Music Group and handed Jim the signed contract. "I'll be back in May," he said. "After I get married. I'll be ready to record then."

Jim flipped a couple of pages. "Twelve songs?"

Owen grinned and tapped his temple. "I've got them up here. I've got three done, plus the one you were sent."

"You know, you could get away with nine songs on the album."

"Nah." Owen felt lighter than he had since arriving in Nashville. "I'm feeling good about twelve." He pointed to the contract. "But I did change the due date. I don't want to rush the way I did last time. I'll be a newlywed and I have a daughter who's about to turn nine. I can't work all the time the way I did last time."

Jim turned to the appropriate page. "December?"

"We can get the album out in February, and I can be playing in March," he said. "I believe the SXSW is still the place to be. You can use a teaser in July to pitch me, and the media will then know that I'm back, making another album."

Jim quirked an eyebrow at him. "Look who's thinking about marketing this time."

"There will be lots of differences this time around," Owen said.

"You think people won't already know about your trip down here? That they won't find out until July?"

"That's exactly what I think," Owen said. "No one knows I'm here except my family. I've stuck to my hotel and your office. I don't want anyone to know until summertime, until I've moved back with my family." He narrowed his eyes at Jim. "Can we make that happen? I don't want reporters at my wedding." He couldn't even imagine how Natalie would react then.

Jim set the contract on his desk. "No one will know until summer." He shook Owen's hand, the deal finally done.

———

Natalie let Julie flutter around her like a hummingbird, her fingers adjusting the veil, then swiping something from her face, then straightening a button. She sniffed as she'd been weeping for most of the morning.

"I can't believe you're getting married," she said. "And to Owen, the boy you've loved your whole life." Julie stepped back and clasped her hands to her heart. "I'm so happy for you."

Natalie received her sister's wet smile and hugged her. "Thank you, Julie. And hey, you brought a date."

"Pish posh," Julie said. "Don't make a big deal out of it."

"So you aren't dating Talbot?"

Julie's smile turned wicked. "Of course I am." She laughed, her tears now completely gone.

A rush of love filled Natalie from top to bottom. "So I guess I should start saving so we can come to Peach Valley for your wedding."

Julie shook her head, but Natalie saw the longing in her eyes before she managed to hide it. "It's your day, sister." She peeked out the crack in the door. "Dad's ready."

Natalie looked at herself in the mirror, her wedding dress slim and fitted to her every curve. Just above the knee it flared, and she smoothed her hands down her thighs to the mermaid part of the dress.

"You look beautiful, baby." Her mom hugged her, deemed her ready, and they made their way to her dad's side. He too kissed her, fondness in every line of his face.

The organ began to play and the doors in front of them opened. Natalie stepped, her eyes first finding Pastor Palmer. She smiled at him, beyond glad he was there, the man she'd grown up learning from.

When her gaze found Owen's, she was lost inside his handsomeness. Those navy eyes, that slate-gray hat, the perfect cut of his black tux. She wanted to take him home with her and never let him go.

And that was exactly what she was going to do.

———

"It's so hot here." Natalie scraped her bangs off her forehead as Owen fitted the key into the lock of the house he'd bought in Nashville. She'd only seen pictures of it, but it was stunning. Two stories high because it had no basement, and the largest Southern porch that had captured Natalie's heart the moment she'd seen the picture.

"Richland/West End is one of the best neighborhoods," Owen said. "You'll get used to the humidity." He turned back to the truck, where Marie kept telling Tar Baby to sit before she'd let him down. "Just let him get down."

Marie stepped back, a dissatisfied look on her face, and Tar Baby jumped from the truck bed and bounded across the sprawling front lawn to Owen. "Well, should we go take a tour?"

Just as she had over the past three weeks since she and Owen had gotten married, Natalie took a deep breath, ready for anything. "Yes, let's go see where we're going to make our life together."

He bent down and kissed her, his touch tender and elec-trifying at the same time. "Come on, baby doll," he said to Marie who had just started up the steps to the front porch. He took Natalie's hand in his left hand and Marie's in his right.

"All right," he drawled, making Natalie's insides warm and gooey. How she loved hearing him say those two words. How she loved *him*.

"This is where we're gonna live." He toed the door open,

and Natalie decided then and there that she didn't care what the house looked like. She had Owen and Marie, and wherever they were, she wanted to be.

———

Read on for a sneak peek at **RIGHT COWBOY, RIGHT TIME** - the next book in the Horseshoe Home Ranch Romance series.

SNEAK PEEK! RIGHT COWBOY, RIGHT TIME CHAPTER ONE

"*O*h, chips!" Caleb Chamberlain swung the overflowing shopping cart around, several boxes of frozen waffles falling off the top. Ty scooped one up and lifted it back over his shoulder like a football.

"Go long!"

Caleb didn't hesitate. His cowboy boots slipped a little on the tile in the grocery store and his injured leg gave him a bit of trouble, but he got his feet under him soon enough. He sprinted down the frozen foods aisle, glancing over his shoulder when he heard Ty grunt.

He put on a burst of speed to be able to get under the waffle box, reaching...reaching until he pulled it in and tucked it under his arm. A laugh spilled from his mouth as he slid to a stop, the old injury in his lower leg and ankle throbbing just a little. The moms with kids stared at him, and one elderly lady Caleb recognized from church frowned.

He tipped his cowboy hat as they went back to selecting milk and eggs and yogurt, then trotted back to where Ty was still picking fallen waffle boxes from the ground. "That was awesome." Caleb balanced the waffle-football on top of their haul. "But we forgot the chips and Gloria is makin' taco soup tomorrow night."

Getting grocery duty in February was every cowhand's dream, so Caleb wasn't overly concerned about hurrying to get the corn chips. He'd probably even suggest he and Ty stop by the deli to get a soft serve cone before they headed back up the canyon to Horseshoe Home Ranch.

No sense in getting back in time to get another assignment. Not in such chilly weather. Even the grocery store had their usually open front area closed today, because the wind howled like it had a personal vendetta against the Montana town of Gold Valley.

Sometimes it felt that way to Caleb, and he wondered why he still lived here. But he couldn't think of anywhere else he'd rather be. His parents lived here; his younger sister cut hair at the salon; his twin brother had only one more year in Michigan to finish his dentistry degree, then he'd return to open a practice.

Caleb had worked at Horseshoe Home since he was fourteen years old, with only a brief hiatus after he recovered from his car accident, and he didn't see anything changing for the next dozen years.

"Pretty girls up ahead," Ty hissed out of the corner of his mouth, causing Caleb to stop using the shopping cart like it was a scooter.

The three girls walking toward them could hardly have graduated from high school. In fact, in Caleb's best estimation, they were probably still *in* high school. Ty, though the same age as Caleb, looked and acted like a teenager, and could probably get away with dating an eighteen-year-old. But Caleb, who looked all of his twenty-six years, could not.

Didn't even want to.

He wasn't really looking for a new girlfriend, not since the disaster that had been Robin Melcher. Oh, no. Caleb was still trying to rebuild what she'd knocked down five years ago, and it wasn't going that well. Definitely better than when he used to drown himself in alcohol, and exponentially better than healing from an accident stemming from his drinking. So his recovery was probably going better than he thought.

Still, he averted his eyes when Ty said, "Afternoon, ladies," and kept on toward the snack food aisle. Ty was exceptionally good at making women feel special, like he'd known them their whole lives. He'd been one of Caleb's best friends growing up, their friendship cemented for life after Caleb had driven himself off the road and into a cement barrier.

Caleb and Ty had actually known most of the available women in Gold Valley his whole life. None of them were interested in him, and Robin's poisoned words flashed through his mind.

You're going nowhere, Caleb Chamberlain.

She had a sweet, sticky, soprano voice that twanged on

his name, even as he pushed her and her parting words to him from his mind.

He was going nowhere, but that wasn't the problem. The real problem was that going nowhere was just fine with him. He didn't want to leave Gold Valley and Horseshoe Home Ranch, even if he dreamed of being a cowboy in warmer Texas or Oklahoma.

He didn't care if no one was interested. He felt content with his life at the moment, and though he needed to get his self-confidence back where it used to be, he knew a woman wouldn't help with that.

"Nathan!"

He glanced up at the mention of his twin's name. He was used to being mistaken for his twin, as they shared the exact same DNA. Same sandy brown hair. Same dark brown eyes. They even walked with an identical gait.

The similarities ended there. Nathan was driven, and successful, and married now with a baby. Caleb had graduated in agricultural sciences while working at the ranch, where…he still worked. He did just fine, in his opinion, but when compared with Nathan, Caleb definitely paled.

Before he could actually locate the source of who'd called Nathan's name, a woman launched herself into his arms.

"Oof," he grunted as he stumbled backward. Without thinking, he put his hands around the woman, mostly to keep himself from falling down. She smelled like flowers and soap, and Caleb's heart pounced into his throat.

She stepped back in a flurry of black hair, which she

smoothed back to reveal even darker eyes and olive colored skin. She wore a lot of black makeup around her eyes, and Caleb thought she looked exotic. He swallowed and found his throat exceptionally dry.

Beautiful and exotic, a dangerous combination to Caleb's bachelor life.

"It's Holly," she said. "Holly Gray?"

The name struck a bell in Caleb's head, but he couldn't place her. "I was Katherine's best friend in high school?"

Katherine—his younger sister.

Ty nudged him, and Caleb's voice thawed enough for him to emit a strangled chuckle. "Oh, right. Katie."

Her eyes searched his. "I didn't know you were back in town."

"Well, I'm not—" Caleb started, his voice muting when Ty thumped him on the back.

"He's back," Ty said.

Caleb usually enjoyed this game of pretend-to-be-some-one-you're-not, but this time he cast Ty a glare. He turned back to Holly, distracted by her curvy hips and slim waist. "I guess I never really left."

She smiled, a short laugh escaping her dark red lips. Caleb couldn't look away, and he realized he hadn't been in a relationship for too long. His brain searched for how long, but it was being slow and dumb.

"It feels that way, doesn't it?" Holly glanced back to where she'd left her cart. "This town does have some sort of magic, though, doesn't it?" She looked at him, and he realized she'd asked two questions.

"Yeah." He answered them both at the same time and immediately cursed himself for sounding like he'd forgotten how to breathe.

"So what brings you back to town?" Ty asked, stepping slightly in front of Caleb.

Caleb had no idea if Holly had actually left town. His life now pretty much existed up the canyon, on the ranch. It always had, but when Robin had left him, he'd made the thirty-minute drive as often as he necessary to procure the liquor he needed to erase her from his mind.

Now, with that behind him, and his leg fully healed, he came down for church if the roads were good and he didn't have chores to do. And, of course, if he pulled grocery duty.

Holly tossed her curls over her shoulder. "Oh, you know. This and that."

Caleb cocked an eyebrow at her. "How long have you been gone?"

"Five years."

Five years, five years. Caleb tried to think of why Holly Gray would've been mixed up with Nathan five years ago. Recalling his brother's life when his own had been so tumultuous was harder than Caleb liked. He'd been really removed from everyone and everything while dating Robin.

It hit him at the same time Holly leaned forward and kissed his cheek. "We should catch up sometime." She gave him a coy smile, turned, and sashayed back to her cart. She didn't turn and look back, something Caleb was grateful for.

He didn't want her to see how he'd gone still, his mouth hanging open. Ty elbowed him and said, "Who was *that?*"

Caleb swallowed as feeling returned to his muscles. "That was Holly Gray," he said in a monotone. "My twin brother's ex-fiancé."

———

By the time Caleb got back to the ranch, unloaded all the food, and helped Ty divvy it all up, his patience had reached it's end. He needed to call Nathan *now.*

Ty had made some suggestions about Holly, none of which Caleb particularly wanted to entertain—except maybe the part where he'd said Caleb should *definitely* call her and *definitely* get caught up with her.

But Caleb needed to talk to Nathan first. He'd left his groceries at the administration lodge, his breath practically freezing in the air before him, and had taken three steps toward his cabin when Jace called his name.

Caleb groaned inwardly, but turned back to the foreman. "Yeah, boss?"

"Any trouble in town?" Jace leaned against the pillar like he didn't feel the negative temperatures. Maybe he didn't.

"No," Caleb said, his voice automatically going up in pitch. "No trouble." He was so used to denying any wrongdoing, and he'd gotten really good at talking his way out of a mess.

"I shouldn't have sent you and Ty together." Jace sighed.

"I knew that." He finally pinned his gaze on Caleb. "Throwing frozen waffles down the aisle? Really?"

"I didn't throw any waffles." Caleb held up his hands. "I swear." A grin tugged at the corners of his mouth, and he worked to flatten them before the all-seeing eye of Jace Lovell could see.

"What about the rumor of two cowboys wrestling in front of the pretzels?" Jace cocked his head to the side.

"That was nothing," Caleb said. "Ty said my ears were stickin' out, and I elbowed him, and he maybe pushed me back. That's it."

"Where are your groceries?" Jace chin-nodded to Caleb's empty hands.

He shifted his feet. "I just needed to...get to the restroom, boss. I'll get 'em in a few minutes."

Jace chewed on the end of a straw, seemingly without a care in the world. Caleb knew that wasn't true, but the boss didn't generally enjoy Caleb's jokes and jabs. "After you put your stuff away, I need you to get on over to the calf barn. Nelson brought in a sick cow, and I need your opinion."

Caleb couldn't keep the groan inside this time, and he hated how it made him sound. "All right," he said. "But didn't you hire a new vet?"

"Sure did." Jace pushed away from the pillar. "But they don't start until Monday."

And Caleb knew Jace wouldn't call them in on Saturday, even if the whole herd went down. Well, maybe if the whole herd went down. But the foreman tried to make sure everyone got a weekend off every now and then, something Caleb appreciated.

Jace looked out over the horizon. "See you in the barn in a few minutes."

Caleb nodded and practically ran to his cabin, which sat fourth in the line. He used to share with a cowboy named Landon Edmunds, but Landon had gotten married a year ago and moved to the horse ranch he'd bought in Utah. For some reason, Jace hadn't assigned anyone else to live with Caleb, and Caleb actually liked the solitude in the evenings.

He washed his hands and took a moment to crank the space heater all the way to high. Then he dialed Nathan, hoping his brother was home from school.

"Little bro," Nathan said by way of greeting.

"You're only older by three minutes," Caleb said, his usual response, a grin crossing his face. He and Nathan had gotten into *so much trouble* growing up. Caleb had loved every minute of sneaking through dark fields, climbing over locked fences, and kissing pretty girls. It had been his brother who'd pulled him from the wreckage of his life, made him promise never to drink again, ordered him to get clean and get happy.

Caleb had accomplished a couple of those things, and most of the time he thought he was happy. Certainly happier than he had been, especially since he'd been going to church.

"What's goin' on?" Nathan asked, and Caleb noted the western slant in his voice, despite the fact that his brother lived in Michigan now. Caleb had often teased him that he must like a long, torturous winter, because Michigan wasn't much better than northern-central Montana.

Now that Caleb had his brother on the phone, he didn't know how to bring up Holly. He swallowed, the words still not there.

"Caleb?"

"I ran into someone today," he started.

"Sounds intriguing." A baby started crying in the background, and Nathan murmured something Caleb couldn't catch. He used the distraction to organize his next statement.

It was Holly Gray. Whatever happened with you guys? He rolled his eyes. Nathan would see through that in two seconds flat. He'd tease Caleb relentlessly if he let on that he was interested in Holly.

He almost scoffed. How could he be interested in Holly? The very idea was ridiculous—especially because she thought he was Nathan.

"Sorry about that," Nathan said. "Eddie's tired."

"I know how he feels." Caleb wiped his hand over his face, reminding himself he still needed to get over to the calf barn and then get his groceries from the administration lodge. The thought of his standard dinner—a banana-bologna sandwich with butter and mayo—made his mouth water.

"So you met someone today."

"Not really met," Caleb said. "I mean, I already know who she is. She grew up with us, but she left town for a while."

"Oh, it's a woman."

Caleb could practically see Nathan as he leaned back, that wide smile on his face. He was sure his next words would wipe it away.

"Well, who is it?" Nathan asked.

"It's Holly Gray."

Nathan made a low, hissing sound. "Holly Gray. Wow."

"She thought I was you."

"And?"

"And she said we should get caught up."

Nathan laughed, but it held undertones of bitterness. "She really is a special kind of crazy."

Caleb's throat felt sticky. "You never told me what happened with you guys."

"She's crazy," Nathan said again, and Caleb was grateful he didn't bring up *why* Caleb didn't know what had happened. "And once I figured it out, I broke it off with her."

"So…if I…I mean, if she and I…." Caleb exhaled, wishing he'd never called Nathan.

"Are you saying you want to go out with her?"

"No," Caleb said. "Not go out with her. Maybe just hang out or something. She seemed fun."

"She was fun," Nathan said. "I'll give her that."

"So you'd be okay with it. If we hung out."

Nathan laughed again, this time the sound much more natural. "Caleb, you're twenty-six-years old. And I'm married and have a son. You can do whatever you want with Holly Gray."

LIZ ISAACSON

"I don't want to do anything with Holly Gray. Just hang out or whatever."

"Right," Nathan said sarcastically. "I know you, Caleb. And Holly is gorgeous. I can put two and two together."

"I—I haven't dated since Robin," Caleb said. It was what he didn't say that would've blown everything wide open. *I haven't dated since I stopped drinking. Haven't had to tell anyone about that. I haven't gone out since the accident. Haven't had to tell a woman why I limp, why my bones know when it's about to snow.*

"Believe me, I know," Nathan said. "Mom talks to me about it every week when I call. She's just about to sacrifice a goat or something to get you married." Caleb snorted. "I mean, I get it. She's worried about you."

"I'm just fine," Caleb said.

"Are you? Keepin' your promise?"

"Yes, Nathan." Caleb hated feeling like he was the younger, irresponsible brother. He knew Nathan meant well, and it did touch Caleb's heart that someone cared about him enough to ask the hard questions. "So...Holly?"

Nathan chuckled. "Always with the one-track mind. Remember that year you wanted to build a tree house? You were out there every day, all summer long."

"It wouldn't have taken as long if you'd have helped," Caleb said.

"Yeah, the floor probably wouldn't have fallen through the first time you walked on it either." Nathan chuckled, and Caleb joined in. "Just don't say I didn't warn you about Holly," Nathan said.

Caleb let his grin spread. "I like a woman who's a little crazy."

———

Holly skipped church on Sunday because she simply couldn't bear to show her face there—yet. Truth was, she hadn't shown her face in church for a while. She used Sundays to work or study—or catch up on much-needed sleep.

She'd prayed and prayed for a different ending with Nathan, and when she didn't get it, her faith had grown cold, turned hard, sunk to the soles of her feet. She knew her mother would ask, and she should've gone, but she couldn't.

So when she showed up at Horseshoe Home Ranch on Monday morning, she hadn't left her house except to get a few groceries and stop by the hardware store for a new showerhead. The one in her rental didn't spray hard enough, and she had a *lot* of hair to wash and condition every day.

Her new boss, the ranch's foreman, Jace Lovell, had said there would be a formal staff meeting in the administration lodge. She'd worried needlessly about being able to find it, because as she came down the snow-packed road and eased her truck around the bend, the lodge lived up to its name. It stood two-stories tall and proud, and had obviously been the homestead in the past.

The present homestead sat a hundred yards west of the

lodge, twice as big and twice as impressive. The road divided the current homestead from the rest of the ranch buildings, including two horse stables, two large equipment sheds, several other barns and outbuildings, and a long row of cowboy cabins.

Her heart stutter-stepped, but she tamed it back to its normal pulse. She was well-qualified for this job. She had a bachelor's degree in veterinarian medicine, and she was only here for eight months to get the required hours she needed to apply for graduate school in large animal care.

Eight months, she repeated like a mantra. She could live in Gold Valley for eight months, drive all the way out to Horseshoe Home for eight months, weather anything for eight months.

She got out of her truck and tugged down the hem of her coat. Not wanting to spend any more time outside than necessary, she hurried toward the administration lodge and up the steps. No one else seemed to be around, and though the sky was barely lighter than twilight, she hadn't gotten the time wrong. The sun just took forever to rise in February.

She entered the building, breathing in with relief at the blast of heated air.

"Holly." Jace waved from a doorway opposite of her. "In here."

She wove through a maze of desks, which gradually gave way to long tables with chairs positioned down the sides where the cowboys obviously ate, as a bottle of ketchup still sat in the middle of one table. Her step was sure and strong as she approached the room. Men's voice filtered out to her, and she froze.

She wasn't early. If anything, they'd been waiting for her. She should've known cowboys got up at the crack of dawn, and an eight-thirty staff meeting meant morning chores were already completed.

Taking a deep breath, she took the few remaining steps to the doorway, a wider swatch of the room coming into view with each passing second. This room held circular tables, all filled with men wearing cowboy hats. Some also wore leather jackets, while some only had on long-sleeved shirts. They all wore jeans and cowboy boots, and the masculine scent of horse and sweat and cologne assaulted her.

"Boys," Jace started and the room quieted. "This is our new veterinarian, Holly Gray."

Twenty-five pairs of eyes landed on her, and she was extremely glad she'd worn the fitted, olive-colored coat. Not that it offered much protection from the gazes of all those men. At least she'd fit in because she wore jeans and boots too.

"Good morning," she said.

"She'll be running our medical clinic this spring, and I expect you all to show her how we do things here at Horseshoe Home."

One of the men leaned toward another and whispered something. They both smiled and chuckled, and Holly found somewhere else to look. She'd been up at the crack of dawn too, thank you very much. Not a lock of hair sat out of place, and her makeup was flawless. Maybe not the most practical when she'd be working with animals all day, but she wanted the cowboys to take her seriously.

Her eyes landed on Nathan Chamberlain, and her face split into a grin. When he'd broken off their engagement five years ago, he'd had two years of college left. Maybe he'd been as devastated as she'd been. Maybe he'd quit school and had been working at Horseshoe Home all this time.

She'd left town, unable to stay in such a small space with him. It had taken her a lot longer than eight months, but she'd let him go. But looking at him now, she wasn't so sure she'd made the right decision. He looked away from her as Jace said she could go ahead and sit. Somehow she got her feet to move, got her knees to bend, got herself out of the spotlight.

SNEAK PEEK! RIGHT COWBOY, RIGHT TIME CHAPTER TWO

*H*olly wasn't sure of all the tasks Jace assigned to his cowhands. She'd worked at a horse boarding farm in Vermont for the last two years, but the facility wan't nearly as large as a cattle ranch. A few stables, a barn, and a lot of land. She'd cared for, fed, and maintained up to forty horses on the site.

But horses weren't enough, and the amount of hours she needed to apply for a graduate program seemed impossible.

Eight months, she told herself as Jace talked about shoeing, and salting, and setting fence lines. He assigned men to fix windmills, and shovel stalls, and feed cows.

"Gloria is serving lunch today," he said. "At the homestead, from eleven to two. Make sure you tell her thank you."

"Yes, sir," some of the boys murmured, and Holly wondered if she was invited to lunch too. Jace hadn't given her an assignment yet—not that she'd heard anyway. Her mind had been churning with the sheer size of this place compared to Steeple Ridge Farm, where she'd worked previously. Heck, this ranch probably had more than forty horses alone, not to mention the cattle.

"Caleb," Jace said. "You're with me and Holly today."

She looked around for Caleb, the name tickling her memory, but no one stood out. The men started talking as they set about their tasks. Several came over to her and tipped their hats, saying, "Ma'am," as they passed. She noticed more than one who let their eyes linger on hers.

Holly smiled and nodded back, her self-consciousness nearly paralyzing until the room emptied. Only then did she breathe a sigh of relief. Then she turned around and came face-to-face with Nathan.

"Nathan," she said, her heart practically beating against her teeth.

He shook his head. "I'm not Nathan. I tried to tell you yesterday."

"This is Caleb," Jace said. "He's my back-up when I need time off or my baby is sick. He's the smartest of us all, too, with a degree in agricultural sciences."

Holly reeled, her feet stumbling backward. "Caleb?"

"Nathan and I are twins," he said. "Remember?" His chocolately brown eyes burned with pure fire, and she couldn't believe she'd been so stupid. Of course Nathan wouldn't be working a ranch. He'd never liked the outdoors much—which was the exact reason she'd gone into veterinarian medicine. Nathan didn't like animals either.

"Of course I remember," she said. "I just...forgot." That

sounded better than saying she'd only ever had eyes for Nathan, despite the fact that he and Caleb were identical twins, despite the fact that she'd been best friends with their little sister growing up.

"Sure, forgot." Caleb rolled his eyes as he walked past her. "Well, we're startin' in the calf barn this morning. We have a situation out there."

She hurried to follow him, baffled at his reaction to her statement about forgetting about him. "A situation?"

"Caleb thinks one of our yearlings has pneumonia," Jace said.

"He does," Caleb said, glancing back at the other man. "He's got all the symptoms."

"Just one cow?" Holly asked.

"Just the one," Jace said. "One of my boys pulled 'im out of the herd on Saturday because he was coughing. Wouldn't eat anything either."

"His temperature is up," Caleb added as he opened the door and stepped into the winter like the cold didn't touch him. "And not just 'cause he's happy to see me." He grinned at his lame joke and skipped down the steps. "He's totally depressed and just sort of lies around," he added.

"So he's not happy to see you at all," Holly teased, unsure of where the words had come from.

Caleb paused and looked at her from underneath his dark brown cowboy hat. "He's *totally sick* of me." A grin made him even more handsome than she thought possible.

"Okay," Jace said. "That's enough."

Caleb threw a laugh into the sky, and Holly wanted to

catch it, hold onto it, hear it when she lay down to sleep at night. Her feelings came with surprise, and she had to remind herself that Caleb was not Nathan, even if they looked exactly alike, right down to the way Caleb's eyes crinkled in the corners when he smiled and the smattering of freckles across his cheeks and nose.

"C'mon, boss," Caleb said. "Better to laugh than cry, right?" He tilted his head to the side as he approached the barn. "I think the yearling's bawling, though. He must be related to you." He ducked into the barn with a chuckle as Holly tried to figure out the joke.

She glanced at Jace, who shrugged one shoulder. "I guess I cry more than I laugh? I don't know. I don't get that one." He entered the barn too, leaving Holly a moment to offer up a spontaneous prayer.

Let me figure out this situation, she thought. She hadn't actually worked with cows as much as she had horses. *One of the reasons you're here*, she told herself as she stepped through the doorway, realizing she'd thought to ask for divine help even though she wasn't sure God heard her.

At least it wasn't as cold inside the barn, but the smell that assaulted her certainly didn't improve her mood or settle her writhing stomach.

———

Caleb waited against the fence where he'd quarantined the yearling, his insides in pure turmoil.

I forgot.

Caleb had always been the more forgettable twin, and he knew it. Knew it and hated it. Everyone gravitated toward Nathan growing up, because Nathan was smart, Nathan was athletic, Nathan was popular.

Caleb, though he looked just like Nathan, didn't play football. Didn't take advanced classes. Didn't care what others thought about him. He'd turned to jokes and pranks to get people—sometimes his own parents—to notice him.

His head ached and he squeezed his eyes closed to get the pain to go away. Didn't work, and he felt hot and steamed from the way his thoughts rotated furiously in his head. He hadn't even been able to come up with a decent joke because of his irritation with Holly.

I forgot.

As if being mistaken for Nathan wasn't enough, now he was being completely forgotten by people he'd grown up with.

He huffed as she neared, and he nodded toward the black yearling, who moaned pitifully. "See the discharge? Doesn't that look like pneumonia to you?"

She cast him a look that held more nerves than challenge, something he remembered her having. "I'll check it out." She eased into the pen and went about checking the calf. "His temperature is elevated," she said, almost to herself. "Nasal discharge, but his lungs seem just—" She jumped back as the cow coughed, but the disgusted look Caleb expected didn't come.

"A cough." She met Jace's eye, once again bypassing Caleb completely. "I think it's not quite pneumonia yet."

Caleb stood straighter. "It's pneumonia."

"How many years of veterinarian school did you complete?" Holly cocked her hip, and Caleb saw that Latina fire in her eyes.

"How many years have you looked after cattle?" He didn't wait for her to answer. He turned to Jace. "It's pneumonia."

"No wonder everyone around here is sick and tired of him." Holly folded her arms as she refocused on the yearling. "It is the beginning of something. It's odd, though. Calves don't usually get pneumonia when they're this old," she said. "I should check the whole herd."

"Can you get him on antibiotics?" Jace asked.

"Yes." Holly climbed the fence this time, and Jace and Caleb moved back to give her room to jump down. "But he should be kept separate from the herd for at least a few weeks." She pulled her phone from her coat pocket and tapped on it. "Where do you—oh, there's only one animal pharmacy in town." She frowned at the screen. "I should've known," she muttered. When she looked up, Caleb couldn't see a hint of her unhappiness. "That'll be ready in a couple of hours. I guess I'll—"

The barn door slamming into the wall cut her off. Caleb turned toward the door at the same time everyone else did. Ty stood there, his chest heaving.

"Boss, you better come quick."

Jace didn't ask a single question before striding down the aisle, Caleb right behind him. "Talk," Jace barked the closer he got.

"There are more sick cows."

An hour later, Caleb once again stood against a fence, this one with a mixture of mud and snow packed in every direction around it. His breath billowed before him and the mud on his jeans had caked and dried, making his pants twice as heavy and infinitely colder.

Jace exhaled loudly as he joined Caleb. "I'll need you to get down to town and get the medicine."

"No problem."

"Take Holly with you."

Caleb felt like Jace had thrown a bucket of water in his face. "What? Why?"

"She can get more medicine than you can, for starters."

"Starters?"

Jace squared his shoulders and turned toward Caleb. "I need you to go with her so she can load her boxes into her truck, and your truck." He spoke slower than usual, and that was saying something.

Caleb squinted at him. "Are you tellin' me she's moving up here?"

"She has half a herd of cows to look after," he said.

"So that's a yes."

"Well, she can't be drivin' back and forth in the winter." Jace started to move away, and Caleb nearly went down on a slick spot of snow in his haste to follow him.

"Why not?" he asked. "People do it all the time, and she has a truck." He didn't want to admit he liked that little fact about her. He didn't know many women who drove a truck, certainly none who had curves like Holly's.

"I need her up here, and she just got to town. She's livin' with her parents." Jace leveled his gaze at him, and Caleb shrank back a step. "So she doesn't have much and hasn't unpacked hardly anything. I need you to go help her load up, get the medicine, and get back up here."

Caleb let Jace go this time, numb inside and out—and not because of the weather.

———

Read RIGHT COWBOY, RIGHT TIME today! A happy-go-lucky cowboy, a fiery veterinarian, and the mistaken identity that sparks a new romance...

BOOKS IN THE HORSESHOE HOME RANCH ROMANCE SERIES:

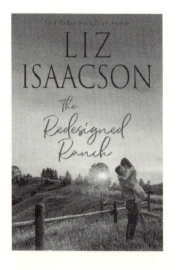

The Redesigned Ranch (Book 1): Jace Lovell, still nursing a wounded heart after being jilted at the altar, has dedicated himself to becoming the best foreman at Horseshoe Home Ranch. When he decides to hire an interior designer to please the ranch owner's wife, he didn't expect to be faced with a familiar face from his past. **Can Belle's patience and faith help Jace find the path to forgiveness and lead them to discover their own slice of happily-ever-after?**

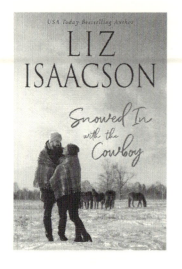

Snowed in with the Cowboy (Book 2): Sterling Maughan, once a renowned snowboarder, is in self-imposed exile at his family cabin after a tragic accident stole his career. Lost and without purpose, solitude is his only companion until an unexpected visitor disrupts his isolation. **Can Norah trust Sterling enough to let him into her life and give their unexpected and forbidden love a chance?**

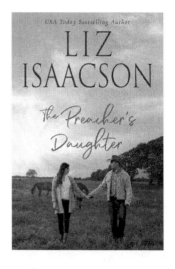

The Preacher's Daughter (Book 3): Landon Edmunds, a cowboy born and bred, has had his rodeo dreams realized and then dashed by a career-ending injury. Back in his hometown working at Horseshoe Home Ranch, he yearns for a new beginning with a ranch of his own. His sights are set on buying a horse ranch to train rodeo horses, but his plans take a detour when his high school best friend, Megan Palmer, steps back into his life. **Will they choose to follow their hearts, or will they let true love slip through their fingers again?**

Be sure to check out the spinoff series, the Brush Creek Cowboys romances after you read THE PREACHER'S DAUGHTER. Start with BRUSH CREEK COWBOY.

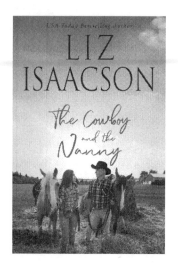

The Cowboy and the Nanny(Book 4): Twelve years ago, Owen Carr traded his roots and his sweetheart in Gold Valley for the bright lights of Nashville, where he found fame as a country music star. But when a tragic accident leaves him single-handedly raising his eight-year-old niece, Marie, he's forced to return home. Overwhelmed and out of his depth, Owen finds a lifeline in a most unexpected place. **As they mend bridges and explore the sparks that still sizzle between them, will they open their hearts to a second chance at love?**

LIZ ISAACSON

Right Cowboy, Right Time

Right Cowboy, Right Time (Book 5): Caleb Chamberlain, a fun-loving cowboy at Horseshoe Home Ranch, has spent the last five years wrestling with the ghosts of his past—a devastating breakup, alcoholism, and a near-fatal accident. Now, he's finally found solace in laughter and the rhythmic simplicity of ranch life. But a chance encounter with a familiar face threatens to upheave his newfound peace. **Can they navigate the shadows of the past to find their happily-ever-after?**

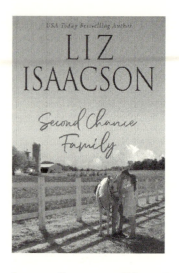

Second Chance Family (Book 6): Ty Barker has been living a carefree existence for the last thirty years. As friends around him found love and started families, Ty filled his time by giving horseback riding lessons and serving on a community service committee. But beneath the jovial surface, he's starting to feel the sting of loneliness. **He knows he wants River Lee in his life—but the question is, can he navigate the delicate steps needed to make her stay with him?**

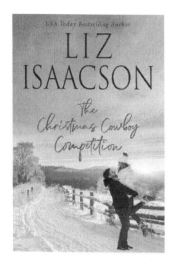

The Christmas Cowboy Competition (Book 7): Archer Bailey has already had to yield one job to Emersyn "Emery" Enders. So when the opportunity of a cowhand job at Horseshoe Home Ranch presents itself, he keeps it to himself. Emery, whose temporary job is ending but whose responsibilities towards her physically disabled sister aren't, is left in the dark.

As the festive season unfolds, **will Emery and Archer navigate the complexities of the ranch, their close living arrangements, and their personal challenges to discover the love building between them? Or will their rivalry rob them of the greatest Christmas gift of all—true love?**

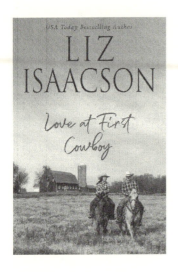

Love at First Cowboy (Book 8): Elliott Hawthorne, a career cowboy, has just witnessed his best friend and cabinmate forsake bachelorhood for matrimony. He'd be joyous if he weren't so green with envy. When a call about a family accident demands his presence, Elliott finds himself rushing from the ranch to his parents' house to see what's going on with his daddy, where he encounters the most stunning woman he's ever laid eyes on. **But as they encounter the complex dynamics of family responsibilities and personal desires, can their love-at-first-sight grow strong enough withstand the test of time?**

BOOKS IN THE BRUSH CREEK COWBOY ROMANCE SERIES:

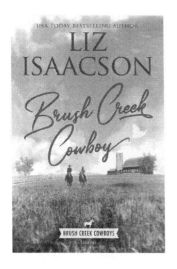

Brush Creek Cowboy (Book 1): Former rodeo champion and cowboy Walker Thompson trains horses at Brush Creek Horse Ranch, where he lives a simple life in his cabin with his ten-year-old son. A widower of six years, he's worked with Tess Wagner, a widow who came to Brush Creek to escape the turmoil of her life to give her seven-year-old son a slower pace of life. But Tess's breast cancer is back...

Walker will have to decide if he'd rather spend even a short time with Tess than not have her in his life at all. Tess wants to feel God's love and power, but can she discover and accept God's will in order to find her happy ending?

The Cowboy's Challenge (Book 2): Cowboy and professional roper Justin Jackman has found solitude at Brush Creek Horse Ranch, preferring his time with the animals he trains over dating. With two failed engagements in his past, he's not really interested in getting his heart stomped on again. But when flirty and fun Renee

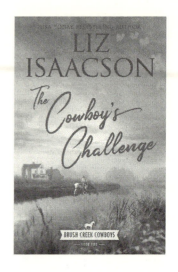

Martin picks him up at a church ice cream bar--on a bet, no less--he finds himself more than just a little interested. His Gen-X attitudes are attractive to her; her Millennial behaviors drive him nuts. Can Justin look past their differences and take a chance on another engagement?

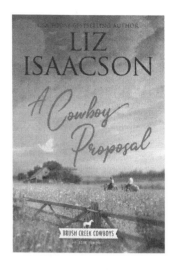

A Cowboy Proposal (Book 3): Ted Caldwell has been a retired bronc rider for years, and he thought he was perfectly happy training horses to buck at Brush Creek Ranch. He was wrong. When he meets April Nox, who comes to the ranch to hide her pregnancy from all her friends back in Jackson Hole, Ted realizes he has a huge family-shaped hole in his life. April is embarrassed, heartbroken, and trying to find her extinguished faith. She's never ridden a horse and wants nothing to do with a cowboy ever again. Can Ted and April create a family of happiness and love from a tragedy?

A New Family for the Cowboy (Book 4): Blake Gibbons oversees all the agriculture at Brush Creek Horse Ranch, sometimes moonlighting as a general contractor. When he meets Erin Shields, new in town, at her aunt's bakery, he's instantly smitten. Erin moved to Brush Creek after a divorce that left her penniless, homeless, and a single mother of three children under age eight. She's nowhere near ready to start dating again, but the longer Blake hangs around the bakery, the more she starts to like him. Can Blake and Erin find a way to blend their lifestyles and become a family?

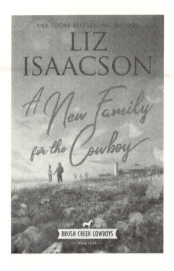

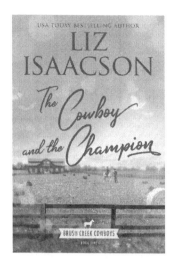

The Cowboy and the Champion (Book 5): Emmett Graves has always had a positive outlook on life. He adores training horses to become barrel racing champions during the day and cuddling with his cat at night. Fresh off her professional rodeo retirement, Molly Brady comes to Brush Creek Horse Ranch as Emmett's protege. He's not thrilled, and she's allergic to cats. Oh, and she'd like to stay cowboy-free, thank you very much. But Emmett's about as cowboy as they come.... Can Emmett and Molly work together without falling in love?

Schooled by the Cowboy (Book 6): Grant Ford spends his days training cattle—when he's not camped out at the elementary school hoping to catch a glimpse of his ex-girlfriend. When principal Shannon Sharpe confronts him and asks him to stay away from the school, the spark between them is instant and hot. Shannon's

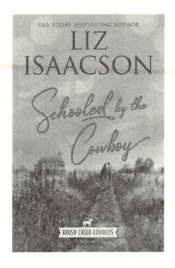

expecting a transfer very soon, but she also needs a summer outdoor coordinator—and Grant fits the bill. Just because he's handsome and everything Shannon's ever wanted in a cowboy husband means nothing. Will Grant and Shannon be able to survive the summer or will the Utah heat be too much for them to handle?

Second Chance Ranch: A Three Rivers Ranch Romance (Book 1): After his deployment, injured and discharged Major Squire Ackerman returns to Three Rivers Ranch, wanting to forgive Kelly for ignoring him a decade ago. He'd like to provide the stable life she needs, but with old wounds opening and a ranch on the brink of financial collapse, it will take patience and faith to make their second chance possible.

Third Time's the Charm: A Three Rivers Ranch Romance (Book 2): First Lieutenant Peter Marshall has a truckload of debt and no way to provide for a family, but Chelsea helps him see past all the obstacles, all the scars. With so many unknowns, can Pete and Chelsea develop the love, acceptance, and faith needed to find their happily ever after?

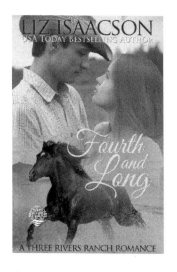

Fourth and Long: A Three Rivers Ranch Romance (Book 3): Commander Brett Murphy goes to Three Rivers Ranch to find some rest and relaxation with his Army buddies. Having his ex-wife show up with a seven-year-old she claims is his son is anything but the R&R he craves. Kate needs to make amends, and Brett needs to find forgiveness, but are they too late to find their happily ever after?

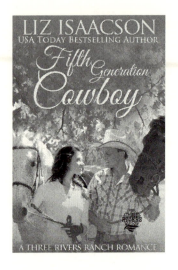

Fifth Generation Cowboy: A Three Rivers Ranch Romance (Book 4): Tom Lovell has watched his friends find their true happiness on Three Rivers Ranch, but everywhere he looks, he only sees friends. Rose Reyes has been bringing her daughter out to the ranch for equine therapy for months, but it doesn't seem to be working. Her challenges with Mari are just as frustrating as ever. Could Tom be exactly what Rose needs? Can he remove his friendship blinders and find love with someone who's been right in front of him all this time?

Sixth Street Love Affair: A Three Rivers Ranch Romance (Book 5): After losing his wife a few years back, Garth Ahlstrom thinks he's ready for a second chance at love. But Juliette Thompson has a secret that could destroy their budding relationship. Can they find the strength, patience, and faith to make things work?

The Seventh Sergeant: A Three Rivers Ranch Romance (Book 6): Life has finally started to settle down for Sergeant Reese Sanders after his devastating injury overseas. Discharged from the Army and now with a good job at Courage Reins, he's finally found happiness—until a horrific fall puts him right back where he was years ago: Injured and depressed. Carly Watters, Reese's new veteran care coordinator, dislikes small towns almost as much as she loathes cowboys. But she finds herself faced with both when she gets assigned to Reese's case. Do they have the humility and faith to make their relationship more than professional?

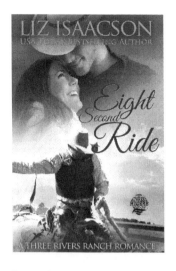

Eight Second Ride: A Three Rivers Ranch Romance (Book 7): Ethan Greene loves his work at Three Rivers Ranch, but he can't seem to find the right woman to settle down with. When sassy yet vulnerable Brynn Bowman shows up at the ranch to recruit him back to the rodeo circuit, he takes a different approach with the barrel racing champion. His patience and newfound faith pay off when a friendship--and more--starts with Brynn. But she wants out of the rodeo circuit right when Ethan wants to rejoin. Can they find the path God wants them to take and still stay together?

The First Lady of Three Rivers Ranch: A Three Rivers Ranch Romance (Book 8): Heidi Duffin has been dreaming about opening her own bakery since she was thirteen years old. She scrimped and saved for years to afford baking and pastry school in San Francisco. And now she only has one year left before she's a certified pastry chef. Frank Ackerman's father has recently retired, and he's taken over the largest cattle ranch in the Texas Panhandle. A horseman through and through, he's also nearing thirty-one and looking for someone to bring love and joy to a homestead that's been dominated by men for a decade. But when he convinces Heidi to come clean the cowboy cabins, she changes all that. But the siren's call of a bakery is still loud in Heidi's ears, even if she's also seeing a future with Frank. Can she rely on her faith in ways she's never had to before or will their relationship end when summer does?

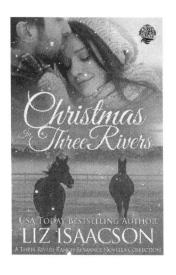

Christmas in Three Rivers: A Three Rivers Ranch Romance (Book 9): Isn't Christmas the best time to fall in love? The cowboys of Three Rivers Ranch think so. Join four of them as they journey toward their path to happily ever after in four, all-new novellas in the Amazon #1 Bestselling Three Rivers Ranch Romance series.

THE NINTH INNING: The Christmas season has never felt like such a burden to boutique owner Andrea Larsen. But with Mama gone and the holidays upon her, Andy finds herself wishing she hadn't been so quick to judge her former boyfriend, cowboy Lawrence Collins. Well, Lawrence hasn't forgotten about Andy either, and he devises a plan to get her out to the ranch so they can reconnect. Do they have the faith and humility to patch things up and start a new relationship?

TEN DAYS IN TOWN: Sandy Keller is tired of the dating scene in Three Rivers. Though she owns the pancake house, she's looking for a fresh start, which means an escape from the town where she grew up. When her older brother's best friend, Tad Jorgensen, comes to town for the holidays, it is a balm to his weary soul. A helicopter tour guide who experienced a near-death experience, he's looking to start over too--but in Three Rivers. Can Sandy and Tad navigate their troubles to find the path God wants them to take--and discover true love--in only ten days?

ELEVEN YEAR REUNION: Pastry chef extraordinaire, Grace Lewis has moved to Three Rivers to help Heidi Ackerman open a bakery in Three Rivers. Grace relishes the idea of starting over in a town where no one knows about her failed cupcakery. She doesn't expect to run into her old high school boyfriend, Jonathan Carver. A carpenter working at Three Rivers Ranch, Jon's in town against his will. But with Grace now on the scene, Jon's thinking life in Three Rivers is suddenly looking up. But with her focus on baking and his disdain for small towns, can they make their eleven year reunion stick?

THE TWELFTH TOWN: Newscaster Taryn Tucker has had enough of life on-screen. She's bounced from town to town before arriving in Three Rivers, completely alone and completely anonymous--just the way she now likes it. She takes a job cleaning at Three Rivers Ranch, hoping for a chance to figure out who she is and where God wants her. When she meets happy-go-lucky cowhand Kenny Stockton, she doesn't expect sparks to fly. Kenny's always been "the best friend" for his female friends, but the pull between him and Taryn can't be denied. Will they have the courage and faith necessary to make their opposite worlds mesh?

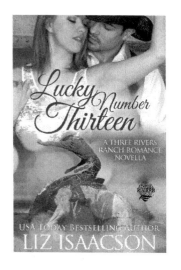

Lucky Number Thirteen: A Three Rivers Ranch Romance (Book 10): Tanner Wolf, a rodeo champion ten times over, is excited to be riding in Three Rivers for the first time since he left his philandering ways and found religion. Seeing his old friends Ethan and Brynn is therapuetic--until a terrible accident lands him in the hospital. With his rodeo career over, Tanner thinks maybe he'll stay in town--and it's not just because his nurse, Summer Hamblin, is the prettiest woman he's ever met. But Summer's the queen of first dates, and as she looks for a way to make a relationship with the transient rodeo star work Summer's not sure she has the fortitude to go on a second date. Can they find love among the tragedy?

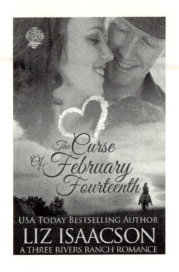

The Curse of February Fourteenth: A Three Rivers Ranch Romance (Book 11): Cal Hodgkins, cowboy veterinarian at Bowman's Breeds, isn't planning to meet anyone at the masked dance in small-town Three Rivers. He just wants to get his bachelor friends off his back and sit on the sidelines to drink his punch. But when he sees a woman dressed in gorgeous butterfly wings and cowgirl boots with blue stitching, he's smitten. Too bad she runs away from the dance before he can get her name, leaving only her boot behind...

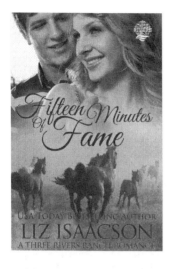

Fifteen Minutes of Fame: A Three Rivers Ranch Romance (Book 12): Navy Richards is thirty-five years of tired—tired of dating the same men, working a demanding job, and getting her heart broken over and over again. Her aunt has always spoken highly of the matchmaker in Three Rivers, Texas, so she takes a six-month sabbatical from her high-stress job as a pediatric nurse, hops on a bus, and meets with the matchmaker. Then she meets Gavin Redd. He's handsome, he's hardworking, and he's a cowboy. But is he an Aquarius too? Navy's not making a move until she knows for sure...

Sixteen Steps to Fall in Love: A Three Rivers Ranch Romance (Book 13): A chance encounter at a dog park sheds new light on the tall, talented Boone that Nicole can't ignore. As they get to know each other better and start to dig into each other's past, Nicole is the one who wants to run. This time from her growing admiration and attachment to Boone. From her aging parents. From herself.

But Boone feels the attraction between them too, and he decides he's tired of running and ready to make Three Rivers his permanent home. **Can Boone and Nicole use their faith to overcome their differences and find a happily-ever-after together?**

The Sleigh on Seventeenth Street: A Three Rivers Ranch Romance (Book 14): A cowboy with skills as an electrician tries a relationship with a down-on-her luck plumber. Can Dylan and Camila make water and electricity play nicely together this Christmas season? Or will they get shocked as they try to make their relationship work?

ABOUT LIZ

Liz Isaacson writes inspirational romance, usually set in Texas, or Wyoming, or anywhere else horses and cowboys exist. She lives in Utah, where she writes full-time, takes her two dogs to the park everyday, and eats a lot of veggies while writing. Find her on her website at feelgoodfiction-books.com

Made in the USA
Coppell, TX
05 February 2025

45494118R00189